"I did

about the house,

Torie explained. "I came on business. As chairperson of the City Council's Greeting Committee, it's my pleasure to officially welcome you to England, Tennessee."

"Oh, really?" Dan muttered.

"And to volunteer my services as hostess, guide and whatever else it might take to make you feel at home."

Dan stood in silence for a moment, a thoughtful look on his face. "Does this mean you've forgiven me for buying the house?"

"Oh, yes," Torie replied with complete honesty. She had—several times.

"And does it mean we're going to be friends?"

Friends? Torie realized with a start that she craved something much more than friendship with Dan Stewart, and the knowledge distressed her. Dan Stewart was *not* husband material in her eyes.

"Oh, of course." She turned to leave, but Dan caught her hand and pulled her back, then wrapped an arm around her, tugging her closer. "What are you doing?"

"Thanking you for your welcoming efforts so far," Dan replied.

Dear Reader:

Welcome to Silhouette Romance—experience the magic of the wonderful world where two people fall in love. Meet heroines who will make you cheer for their happiness and heroes (be they the boy next door or a handsome, mysterious stranger) who will win your heart. Silhouette Romance novels reflect the magic of love—sweeping you away with stories that will make you laugh and cry; heartwarming, poignant stories that will move you time and time again.

In the next few months, we're publishing romances by many of your all-time favorites such as Diana Palmer, Brittany Young, Annette Broadrick and many others. Your response to these authors and other authors in Silhouette Romance has served as a touchstone for us, and we're pleased to bring you more books with Silhouette's distinctive medley of charm, wit and—above all—*romance.*

During 1991, we have many special events planned. Don't miss our WRITTEN IN THE STARS series. Each month in 1991, we're proud to present readers with a book that focuses on the hero—and his astrological sign.

I hope you'll enjoy this book and all of the stories to come. Come home to romance—Silhouette Romance—for always!

Sincerely,

Tara Gavin
Senior Editor

LINDA VARNER

A House Becomes a Home

Published by Silhouette Books New York
America's Publisher of Contemporary Romance

Dedicated to
Sally Hawkes, Penny Richards and Terri Herrington,
who shared their time and talent
and somehow made a writer out of me.
To Helen Myers, who keeps my spirits up.
And to Phyllis Krieger,
who never doubted for a moment that I could do it.

SILHOUETTE BOOKS
300 E. 42nd St., New York, N.Y. 10017

A HOUSE BECOMES A HOME

ISBN: 0-373-08780-2

First Silhouette Books printing March 1991

Printed in the U.S.A.

Books by Linda Varner

Silhouette Romance

Heart of the Matter #625
Heart Rustler #644
Luck of the Irish #665
Honeymoon Hideaway #698
Better To Have Loved #734
A House Becomes a Home #780

LINDA VARNER

has always had a vivid imagination. For that reason, while most people counted sheep to get to sleep, she made up romances. The search for a happy ending sometimes took more than one night, and when one story grew to mammoth proportions, Linda decided to write it down. The result was her first romance novel.

Happily married to her junior high school sweetheart, the mother of two and a full-time secretary, Linda still finds that the best time to plot her latest project is late at night when the house is quiet and she can create without interruption. Linda lives in Conway, Arkansas, where she was raised, and believes the support of her family, friends and writers' group made her dream of being published come true.

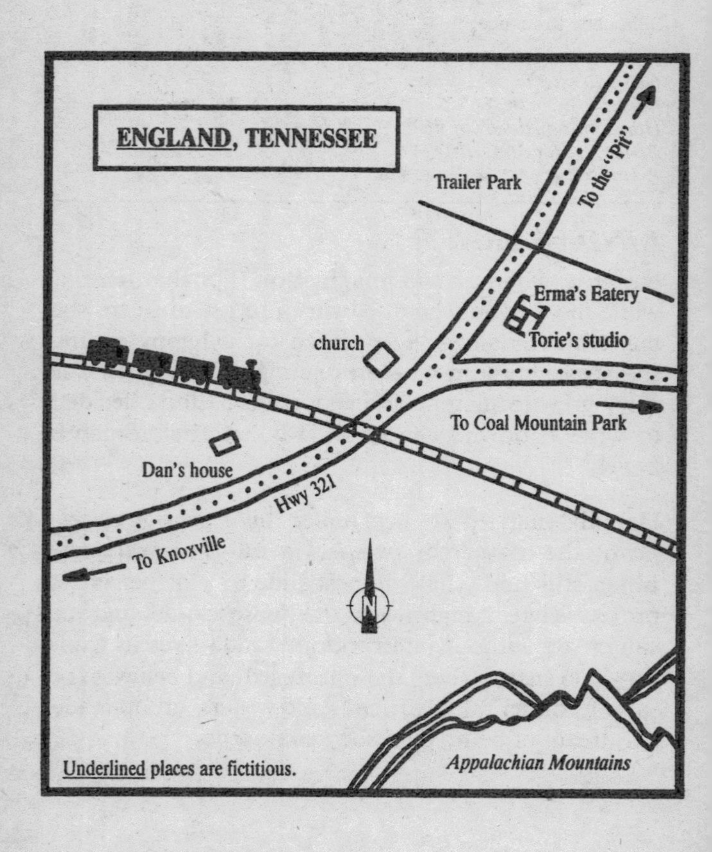
ENGLAND, TENNESSEE
Trailer Park
To the "Pit"
Erma's Eatery
church
Torie's studio
To Coal Mountain Park
Dan's house
Hwy 321
To Knoxville
N
Underlined places are fictitious.
Appalachian Mountains

Prologue

Sixteen-year-old Danny Stewart leaned to his right, pressing his forehead and cheek to the glass of the window as though that might enable him to see what lay around the curve ahead of the chugging train. He knew it wouldn't be long until that wonderful old house came into view. He smiled with anticipation. Would it still be there? Would it look the same?

"Better get ready, son. England's just around the bend."

Danny straightened up immediately and glanced over at his beloved dad, engineer of this picturesque tourist train. At John Stewart's nod of encouragement, Danny reached out to grasp the microphone. He cleared his throat, flipped a switch and then put the instrument to his mouth.

"Your attention, please," he said, enunciating each word with care and pride. "We're now approaching England, Tennessee, the first of many beautiful settlements we'll see on our journey through the Appalachians today.

England has a population of fifteen hundred and is the home of Coal Mountain, our state's oldest theme park."

Danny flicked off the mike and turned to his companion. "How was that?"

"Great," his dad said with a broad grin. He reached out, playfully tugging the bill of Danny's striped engineer's hat, which was just like his own. "You've turned out to be one heck of a guide."

A warm glow spread through Danny at those words. He sighed his contentment with summertime fathers and old-time trains, then glanced back out the window. Of necessity they had slowed to pass through the area. Danny looked anxiously forward again, knowing at any minute he would be able to see that little yellow house he'd grown to love during these summers spent with his dad. Though nothing more than a rather ordinary frame house a few miles out of town, the two-story structure symbolized exactly what Danny wanted most in this life: the security of home and family.

He closed his eyes, picturing how he hoped the house would look—how it *had* looked every day the previous summer. He envisioned the vegetable garden on one side, the huge oak tree with its rope swing on the other. On that swing he imagined he saw the little girl, looking the same as she always did, but with a year's growth on her. Her long, white-gold curls fanned out behind her, capturing the rays of the morning sun as her mother, or sometimes her father, lovingly swung her back and forth. They would hear the train's whistle and run to the picket fence. They'd laugh with delight and wave so big. . . .

Heart suddenly aching with envy, Danny opened his eyes to dispel the happy scene. The train topped a rise. The roof of the old house and then the rest of it appeared. Danny saw the towering tree and the swing . . . the *empty* swing.

Where is she? he wondered, anxiously scanning the grassy yard, the fence, the dirt road.

Where is she?

Chapter One

Where is she?

Dan Stewart heard the sixth and final peal of the bell in the old church down the road and growled his displeasure. She was an hour late. She was supposed to meet him at five o'clock sharp and it was already six. Nothing on earth irritated him more than a woman who couldn't be on time. He was never late himself, a compulsion resulting from years of living by schedules—first the navy, and most recently traveling the NASCAR circuit as a race-car driver.

Where the hell is she?

Dan stepped out of his truck and slammed the door, venting his impatience. He paced on the damp grass next to the gleaming black vehicle and the trailer attached to it. His gaze flicked restlessly over the western horizon. He saw no signs of life and turned back, once again perusing the broken-down fence and weathered house before him—sadly neglected remains of a vision that had haunted him since childhood.

He half smiled to himself and strode over to a brightly painted sign, planted deep in rich Tennessee mud. He ran his hand over the letters on it, still not quite believing his eyes or his good fortune.

For Sale.

Dan tossed his head back and laughed aloud, a sound of triumph the October wind caught and dispersed into a threatening sky. His laughter soon faded but not his smile, as precious memories washed over him. He thought about those wonderful summers he'd spent with his father after his parents split—four of them before the fatal heart attack. He remembered the daily ride on the Tennessee tourist train that his dad engineered.

He also remembered a little towheaded girl who swung on a rope swing, waved at trains and probably took for granted the things he'd lost and would never have again. What had happened to her? To her parents? Had the all-American family simply outgrown the old frame structure and bought a more modern one somewhere? Or had some kind of misfortune claimed their happiness, leaving only this pitiful monument to the good life?

Not the latter, Dan hoped, immediately reminding himself that it didn't really matter. For whatever reason, they were obviously long gone now and the house was his.

His.

Yes, the Fates had finally smiled on Daniel Stewart. He was footloose, fancy-free, solvent. And, as of three o'clock that very afternoon, he was also the proud owner of the most wonderful house in Tennessee.

Wonderful? Probably to no one but him, he realized, eyeing it more critically but with love. Suddenly in better spirits, Dan decided to make the best of the time alone to walk the boundaries of the land he'd just purchased, so he could tag the corner markers—if he could find them in the overgrown weeds. But before he could manage a step, a late-model sedan topped the rise and took the turn into the long drive on two wheels. The vehicle crunched to a halt at the end of it, spraying gravel and mud everywhere.

"Now who in the heck is *he?*" Victoria Hanover muttered to herself as she turned off the motor of her car. She peered through the window to study the dark-haired stranger leaning so nonchalantly against that monster of a truck, his eyes trained on her. Having lived all twenty-two years of her life in England, Torie knew each and every male within walking, hitching or driving distance. This particular specimen, with his straight nose, kissable lips and firm, almost shaved jawline, was a sight to behold and definitely, but *definitely,* no one she knew.

Curiosity piqued, she dragged her gaze from his long, denim-covered legs to the license plate on his vehicle. Florida. That explained that, but what was he doing standing in front of the house she intended to buy? Surely he wasn't interested in it?

But of course not. The structure, which was the rental property of a man who lived in Nashville, had been placed on the market only at nine that very morning. Her best friend, Patty, a part-time agent at the one and only realty company in town, had called her first thing. They hadn't even run an ad on it yet.

And where was Patty, anyway? Torie, who'd spent most of her day in the neighboring town of Hankins, hadn't talked to her since early that morning when they had set up a meeting. She glanced at her watch, noting it wasn't quite six-fifteen. Her old friend still had a few minutes left before she could be considered late—just enough time for Torie to try to find out what tall, dark and handsome was doing hanging around *her* house. Then she'd send him on his way or, if she was lucky, put him on hold until she and

Patty had scouted the place. Torie hadn't set foot in it in years. She needed Patty's expert opinion of its current state in order to make a fair, yet affordable offer. That in mind, Torie climbed quickly out of the car.

"Hello there," she called, waving.

Dan nodded coolly in response to her greeting. Just as coolly, he eyed the shapely young woman. Leggy and slender, she wore a tropical-print wraparound skirt over what appeared to be a hot pink leotard, hardly appropriate attire for a business appointment, to his way of thinking, but then, arriving an hour late wasn't exactly what he'd call professional, either.

With a toss of long, honey-gold hair she gave the door an equally unprofessional but oh-so-sexy nudge with her hip and then headed in his direction, skillfully sidestepping a mud puddle in her path.

Not quite sure what to make of her, Dan stood in silence as she approached. He tried to think of the name the owner of the agency had given him. Was it Sylvia? Sandra?

"I've been waiting for you since five o'clock," he said when she reached him, refusing to respond to her sunny smile.

"Well, darn," she replied, her big, blue eyes dancing with mischief. "I was hoping you'd been waiting all your life."

Startled by such teasing from a stranger who might not be who he'd thought she was, Dan barely managed to stammer, "Aren't you from Winters Realty?"

Her smile vanished. "No. Are you waiting for someone from there?"

"Yeah," he said. "An agent, and she's very late."

"I take it you're interested in the property, too."

Too? She didn't know that the property had already been sold? Dan frowned, "You're here to look at the house?"

"That's right." Her gaze boldly swept over him from head to toe and then back up again, as though she were taking measure of the competition. "And I'm supposed to be meeting one of Winters's agents here at six-fifteen—Patty Millsap. Who did you talk to?"

"I talked to the owner of the agency, actually," Dan said, for some reason reluctant to reveal that the conversation had taken place at the bank, when he'd sighed papers for the house. "He told me he'd send someone out. I can't seem to remember her name, but I think it started with an *S*."

"Susan?"

"That's it—Susan."

Great. Torie thought, heart sinking. Susan Winters, the agency owner's niece, was Patty's arch rival. Obviously she was trying to get the jump on Patty *and* spite Torie at the same time. That wasn't really surprising, since there was no love lost between them and this piece of property was one of the few presently for sale in the little town.

But how on earth had Susan found this prospective buyer so quickly? He was from Florida, for heaven's sake—a foreigner. Torie, who had wanted the house ever since her mother sold it seventeen years ago, hadn't even expected local competition in her bid for ownership.

And why should she? It had been on the market twice since then and never sold. How could she have known that this time, when she finally had the wherewithal to actually make an offer, someone would show up wanting to buy it, too? Puzzled by the development, Torie let her speculative gaze travel over the stranger again. She noted, with grudging approval, his faded chambray shirt, leather jacket and snug-fitting jeans. If she added his tawny brown eyes to that, he was nothing short of gorgeous. From the looks of that awesome truck and the rig behind it, he was well-to-do, too.

Now why would a man who looks like *that* be interested in a house that looks like *this?* she wondered, automatically shifting her gaze to the seventy-five-year-old dwelling, which had stood vacant for nearly a year. Though structurally sound, the house needed repairs. Most of the shingles were gone with the wind, as were all the shutters but one, which hung by a single nail on the unpainted wood siding. The roof undoubtedly leaked, and on top of that, the place didn't even have city water or sewers.

Torie looked at him again, frowning thoughtfully. "Would you mind answering a personal question?"

"Ask me, and I'll let you know."

"Why would you want to buy a run-down house on an acre of land in the middle of nowhere?"

His eyes narrowed in obvious provocation. "Why would *you?*"

"I asked you first."

"All right, then, *I* plan to live in it."

"You're kidding!" she exclaimed, eyes rounding in disbelief.

"I need a place to hole up in the winters," Dan retorted defensively. "And I've always dreamed of living in the country."

She bubbled with laughter at that. "Man-oh-man, are you *ever* in the country! Why, the nearest shopping mall is twenty-five miles away, and the Chief of Police here rolls the streets up at ten sharp—"

"Exactly what I'm looking for," Dan snapped to discourage further derogatory comments about his paradise. At once, he wished he hadn't been quite so candid. It was none of her business, anyway, and now she probably thought he was some kind of nerd.

"I see." After an awkward pause, the woman cleared her throat, wet her bottom lip with the tip of her tongue and smiled pityingly at him. "Then England will be perfect for you."

Dan winced. Sure enough, she thought he was a nerd. That rankled. As a winning race-car driver, he'd become used to being viewed as a hero of sorts...especially by the fairer sex.

"I guess we should introduce ourselves," he blurted in an attempt to set things straight. "I'm Dan Stewart." He extended his hand, waiting for her to recognize his name.

She took, shook and released it, her expression never changing. "Victoria Hanover, but please call me Torie."

So much for saving his rep. Obviously she wasn't into auto racing, had probably never even heard of the Winston Cup, much less the race next week in Charlotte. Put firmly in his place, Dan dared not open his mouth again.

"Um, how did you find the place?" she finally asked a few moments later, breaking what had become a weighty silence. "It's not exactly on the beaten path."

What could he say? That he'd fallen in love with an old house he'd viewed from a passing train twenty years ago? That he'd driven two-hundred miles out of his way today just to see if it was still standing, found it for sale and bought it, all in the space of a few hours? Of course not. She would then consider him sentimental, impetuous *and* a nerd.

"Just lucky, I guess," he said, determined to end her inquisition. He had a couple of dozen questions of his own to ask before he would take great pleasure in breaking the news that he'd beaten her to the punch. "Now what about you? Why are you interested in the place?"

"Because I used to live in it when I was a kid," she said with a shrug.

Used to live in it?

Dan's knees threatened to buckle with the shock of her revelation. At once as breathless as a man who'd been punched in the gut, he made closer inspection of Torie's sparkling eyes, uptilted nose, full lips. He took special note of her golden hair, which could well have been silvery-blond at one time, and then tried to guess her age. She looked to be in her early twenties, just about right, but surely, *surely* the odds of this woman actually being the child he had envied so long ago were at least a zillion to one.

Or were they? Dan's heart began to thud erratically when he realized he might actually be face to face with the little girl of his memories, a girl whose family home he'd just purchased...right out from under her. Suddenly feeling a little sick, he decided he had to know for sure.

"No kidding?" he murmured with a casualness that belied his inner turmoil. "Then maybe you could answer some of my questions about the property and the area in general."

"Maybe," she agreed, clearly not thrilled by the idea.

Dan swallowed hard and somehow mustered up a smile. "That's great. I've got a good idea of the boundaries of the lot, but I'd really like to locate the corner markers. Do you have any idea of their exact location?"

"Yes," she told him. "Got on your walking shoes?"

He glanced down at his worn loafers. "Yeah."

"Then why don't I show you . . . ?"

Torie led the way to a spot about ten feet from the road and five feet outside the gaping remains of the picket fence. Kneeling, she swept her hand through the ankle-high grass, digging around until she located a metal stake, which she showed him. Then she stood and pointed eastward before heading that way with purposeful strides. Deciding to hold off on actually tagging the marker, Dan drew out his pocket knife and quickly trimmed the grass and wildflowers so that the stake was easily visible before he loped to catch up with her.

"The last time I was in the area for any length of time—summer about seventeen years ago—the population was actually larger than it is now," he commented. "What happened?"

"Several things," Torie told him, searching her brain for some clever way to discourage Dan Stewart from making an offer on the house. She intended to make use of their time alone to talk him out of moving to her hometown—at least to this particular house—even at the risk of appearing disloyal to her roots. "First was the close of Coal Mountain, the theme park that used to be our main source of income. Ever heard of it?"

"I've heard of it."

"Well, losing the tourist trade and jobs the park generated started the ball rolling," Torie continued. "Then about two years ago the chemical plant over in Rush was shut down—waste-disposal problems. Three-fourths of the citizens of England suddenly found themselves unemployed. Some of the younger families have cleared out since then, leaving mostly retired couples and a few diehards."

"Is that what you are? A diehard?" Dan asked, hooking a thumb through the belt loop of his jeans as he walked along beside her. Torie stopped so abruptly he passed right by her and had to backtrack to hear her answer.

"Yes," she told him. "And unless you are, too, you'll never survive in this sleepy little town."

"Maybe some new blood might revive it," he retorted. Without another word, he pivoted to resume their trek.

Torie huffed her dismay and followed. So much for painting a gloomy picture. All she'd managed to do was irritate this Dan Stewart guy, who didn't seem to like her much. Well, she wasn't wild about him, either, yet had no choice but to stick around. She couldn't give up the house without a fight, not after all these years of longing for it.

"How large is the lot?" he asked, peering back over his shoulder at her.

"Just over an acre now," she told him, hurrying to catch up. "Used to be much larger."

"It's in a very pretty location." His eyes swept the surrounding area, lingering on the Appalachian mountains, which loomed in the distance, splashed with the colors of autumn. "Nice view. It'll be beautiful in winter."

"Yeah. Almost makes up for the lack of amenities."

He arched a dark eyebrow. "Lack of amenities?"

She shrugged. "I'm afraid so."

"Care to expound on that?"

With pleasure, she thought, hiding a grin of triumph at this opportunity to accentuate the negative aspects of country living. "Well, I don't want to discourage you from settling here, of course, but you should know there's no natural-gas line."

"Really?"

"Nope. You have to buy propane and then keep the tank filled. Cable TV doesn't quite make it this far out, either."

"Oh yeah?" He was frowning now. Torie's spirits lifted.

"Yeah. And there's no city water."

"No city water?"

"No," she replied. "There's a well, though...if it hasn't gone dry. The pump is in the well house over there."

"That little building by the tree?"

"That's the one," she said.

"I thought maybe that was the outhouse," he commented.

The outhouse! England might not be Miami, but it wasn't *that* backward! Insulted, Torie opened her mouth to set him straight and quick. Just in time, she spotted the smile teasing the corner of his lips. He hadn't been fooled for a minute. He knew she was trying to put him off buying the place. How embarrassing.

Red-faced, mustering what dignity she could, Torie abruptly abandoned her big plans to discourage him and stepped up the pace. Dan followed her lead. Together and in silence, they covered the remaining distance to the eastern corner of the lot. There she bent down to locate the second buried stake, which she showed to Dan. While he trimmed the weeds all around, she stood upright to get her bearings. Moments later they were moving south in a path parallel to the railroad tracks a few yards to their left, and the picket fence, several more to their right.

"Anything else I should know?" he asked.

Certain he was making fun of her again, Torie flicked a sideways glance in his direction. All traces of his humor had vanished, however, and somewhat encouraged, she tried one more time to get rid of him. "The nearest doctor is fifteen miles east. The nearest hospital, twenty-five."

"Do you have nine-one-one access?"

"Yes, but—"

"Then help is probably never more than minutes away, right?"

She sighed her frustration with his optimism. Her own lay trampled in the grass a few feet back. "If you're lucky."

"I already told you that I am." He smiled. "What else do I need to know?"

"If you want to stay informed, you'll have to drive into town to pick up the newspaper—unless you don't mind getting it in the mail a day late."

"England has a newspaper?" He sounded surprised.

She bristled. It was one thing for her to insult her hometown, quite another for him to. "We have a small but excellent newspaper. Comes out every two weeks."

"That's great. Do you have schools?"

"Of course we have schools *and* one of the best basketball teams in the state."

"I see. Do you have churches?" he next asked.

"Several."

"And a grocery store?"

"Two of them."

"A Laundromat? A car wash?"

"Both."

"What else do you have?"

"A beauty shop, a café, a hardware store and a dance school," she answered proudly.

"And I'll bet anything else I could possibly need is only a twenty-minute drive away. Right?"

"Right," she agreed with a brisk nod.

He grinned. "I told you England is exactly what I'm looking for."

Exactly what he was looking for? England? Belatedly Torie realized that he was the clever one, easily manipulating her into singing the praises of her hometown. Clearly there was more here than met the eye. The man had brains as well as beauty, and for whatever reason, he wanted *her* house.

Damn him.

Suddenly certain she was going to have to know more about her foe before she could conquer him, Torie said, "I noticed your Florida car tags. What city are you from?"

"Daytona Beach."

"Ah, Daytona. My brother went there once with some friends. He still talks about how gorgeous it was."

"Daytona *is* a beautiful city," Dan agreed.

"Too bad you had to leave it," she prompted, in hopes he would open up and reveal his reasons for doing so.

"Yeah, too bad."

Torie waited for more, but silence reigned. "Job transfers are just awful, aren't they?"

"So I've heard."

"You weren't transferred to Tennessee?"

"No."

"But you do plan on settling here?"

"Right here, actually. In England, in this house."

Suddenly at the end of her rope and angered by his arrogant predication, Torie abandoned her line of questioning and stomped ahead.

"Aren't you going to ask me why I chose this particular town?" Dan called after her.

Torie spun to face him, her hands on her hips. "Would you actually tell me, if I did?"

"Hell, I'll tell you even if you don't," he snapped. "I chose this town because I believe it's what life is all about. I intend to live here to a ripe old age."

"Alone?"

"I might buy myself a good dog."

"Well, it's a darn good thing you prefer dogs to women," Torie said.

"What's that supposed to mean?"

"It means that eligible members of the opposite sex are another amenity sadly lacking around here."

"No problem. Since I'm not the marrying kind, I definitely prefer to grow old alone."

"Fine, then. You do that . . . but in somebody else's house."

He shook his head. "No way, honey. It has to be this one."

"But why?" she demanded in exasperation. "Why this one?"

"Because I've dreamed of this house since I was a kid, Torie Hanover."

"But I was born in it," she replied, positive he hadn't meant that literally. "And that means I have more right to it than you do."

Their gazes locked. Disturbed by his searching look, Torie whirled abruptly and left him. A few feet away, she stopped, marked the position of the house in relation to the road and walked a few more steps before squatting down to look for the third metal marker. She pointed it out to Dan, who dropped to one knee beside her to trim the grass with his knife. Leaving him to his task, Torie headed due west, parallel to the graveled road. Dan jumped up, catching her in two long strides.

"Hey, wait," he said, grabbing her hand just as a train's warning whistle sounded from some distance away.

Torie twisted free, deliberately stepping away from him so she could see down the track. She spotted the familiar black engine of the same old-time tourist train, which had traveled the tracks for as long as she could remember.

"There's something I have to tell you," Dan said, stepping into her line of vision again. "But first there's something I have to know."

She ignored him, craning her neck to watch the train, about a half a mile away and fast approaching.

"Torie, listen to me," he said, this time grabbing her by the shoulders. "When did you move out of the house?"

She dragged her gaze from the train. "When my dad died. I was five. My big brothers were not interested in farming, and Mom couldn't keep the place up alone. We moved into a smaller house in town."

"But how long ago?" he persisted.

Torie opened her mouth to answer, but her words were drowned in another blare of the train's whistle, this time mere yards away. Unable to resist a lifelong love of locomotives, she ducked out of Dan's hold and stepped around him, throwing her arm up to wave enthusiastically at the engineer.

The man tipped his black-and-white striped hat and waved back. Then the engine topped the ridge and rounded the curve, noisily trailed by a half dozen passenger cars and a bright red caboose. Enchanted as always, Torie stood in a trance-like state until the last car disappeared from view and left her far behind. Then she sighed softly in contentment. "Boy, does that take me back."

When Dan didn't reply, Torie turned to find him staring at her, face ashen, eyes wide with shock.

"What is it? What's wrong?" she instantly demanded, reaching out to lay a hand on his arm.

"Nothing," he said, shaking off her touch.

"But you look as though you've seen a ghost."

"Yeah? Well, I guess I have," he muttered with a shaky laugh. "I guess I have."

all motivations clear why they each want the house & a attraction between them

14 Pages

Chapter Two

Torie opened her mouth to respond to Dan's astonishing reply, but never had the chance because a car she knew well topped the rise and wheeled into the drive. Patty, a petite redhead, and Susan Winters, a shapely brunette, leaped out of the vehicle and hurried across the yard.

"Dan Stewart?" Susan asked, panting, when she and Patty reached them.

He nodded.

Nudging Torie aside, the brunette extended her hand to him. "I'm Susan Winters, with Winters Realty. Sorry I'm late, but we couldn't find the house key anywhere. I hope the delay hasn't inconvenienced you."

"No harm done, I guess," he said, shaking her hand. "Did you ever locate it?"

"Oh yes," Susan replied, digging into her pocket. "As it turned out, Patty, here, had it all the time." She dragged her adoring gaze away from Dan long enough to glare over her shoulder at her co-worker, then handed him the key. "There you are, and welcome to England."

Welcome to England?

Torie caught her breath and glanced sharply at Patty, whose woebegone expression confirmed that the incomprehensible had happened. There would be no restoration of the house, no reunion of a family scattered to the four winds, no resurrection of the good times.

Dan Stewart had already bought the house.

Stunned to her toes, not quite able to accept the terrible truth, Torie shifted her gaze to Dan, then immediately closed her eyes to block the sight of him standing there, tall and triumphant, against the backdrop of her shattered dreams. At once, reality hit her like a tidal wave and she swayed with the impact.

Muttering an exclamation of concern, Dan reached for her, but she held him at bay with her upraised hand. For all his show of consideration now, he'd played her for a fool only moments before by not telling her the truth. Not for anything would Torie reveal the depth of her despair to him.

"Looks as though I'm a day late and a dollar short," she said instead, somehow forcing a light laugh. "Congratulations. You really *are* a lucky man, Mr. Stewart. Now if you two will excuse me..." Motioning for Patty to follow, Torie pivoted and headed for her car.

"Don't go yet," Dan called after the two of them. "We need to talk."

"Can't it wait?" Susan whined. "It's almost dark, and Uncle James suggested I might want to walk through the house with you tonight to discuss modernization. I do some interior decorating on the side, and I have some wonderful ideas. If we don't get started right away, we'll have to use a flashlight or wait until tomorrow."

So he'd bought the house without so much as a look inside and was already talking "modernization." Torie couldn't believe it, and outrage, intense and fortifying, supplanted her disappointment. With an exclamation of sheer fury, she lunged for her car, Patty scurrying behind. A heartbeat later they were both inside the vehicle.

"I'm so sorry, honey," Patty immediately blurted. "I tried all day to get hold of you."

"It doesn't matter."

"I called your studio, your mom's café, the—"

"It doesn't matter!"

Impatiently swiping at the tear that belied that claim, Torie reached for the key still in the ignition and gave it a twist to start the engine. A backward glance at the house revealed Dan moving toward her car with long-legged strides. Torie stomped on the accelerator in response, leaving him, Susan and the dreams of a lifetime behind her.

"Are you okay?" Patty asked softly a couple of miles later.

"I'm fine," Torie replied, for once oblivious to the beauty of the picturesque church, the farmhouses and the rolling pastures bordering that familiar stretch of highway.

"You don't look fine," Patty persisted.

"I am just the same."

"Are you angry with me?"

"Don't be silly."

"Positive?"

"Of course I'm positive." Torie took one look at Patty's worried face and reached out to give her hand a reassuring squeeze. "I know there's nothing you could have done to stop him."

"That's for darn sure," Patty muttered. "It happened too fast. Why, that For Sale sign hadn't been in the yard an hour before he called the office, and by three this afternoon the place was his."

"How on earth did they get the mortgage papers drawn up so fast?"

"What mortgage? The man paid cash."

Torie's jaw dropped. "You're kidding."

"I would never, ever kid about anything as serious as this," the redhead replied.

"Damn. He must be some kind of loaded."

"Yeah. Apparently that's what winning the Winston Cup will do for you."

"He races?" Torie asked, surprised.

"Races *and* wins," Patty told her. "Didn't you catch his name? That's *Dan Stewart,* honey. *The* Dan Stewart."

"Doesn't ring a bell," Torie responded with a thoughtful frown. "And no wonder. I haven't been to an auto race since the twins left for college over ten years ago."

"That's no excuse for not recognizing him. Why, you probably saw a Lobo 4x4 commercial on television last night."

Torie nearly ran the car off the road. "He does those?"

"Does he ever," Patty replied. "Have you seen the latest one, where he's stretched out on the hood of his truck with his back against the windshield? Just thinking about it makes this little ol' heart of mine go pit-a-pat. I can't imagine your being face to face with those pecs and not recognizing them."

"He had his shirt on today," Torie caustically reminded her.

"That's true," Patty agreed. "And his sunglasses off." She sighed lustily. "Can you believe he's really moving to England? I wonder if he's married."

"It doesn't matter if he is or not," Torie snapped as she wheeled into Patty's drive and hit the brake. "*You* are."

Her friend glanced out her window at a tiny frame house some twenty feet away and the bear of a man sitting on the front porch, open newspaper across his lap. "Oh yeah," she murmured with a sheepish grin, waving to him.

"And if that's not enough to discourage you," Torie continued, "just remember where Mr. Stewart is going to be living when he moves to town."

"I haven't forgotten," Patty said. "How could I? You've wanted to buy that house back since your mama sold it all those years ago. I just can't believe things turned out this way."

Torie couldn't believe it, either. Suddenly bursting into the tears she'd fought for miles, she hid her face in her hands and gave in to her despair. Patty's tears of sympathy immediately joined hers, and it was several moist moments later before either could speak again.

"I hate him, I hate him," Torie sobbed as she accepted the tissue Patty handed her.

"Torie Hanover!" her companion exclaimed, clearly aghast. "You don't know him well enough to hate him."

"And never will."

"Never say never," Patty cautioned. "That just challenges the Fates."

"But it's true. If that man lives in England to his dying day, I'll not speak to him again."

"Torie, honey, lighten up," Patty said, a frown of genuine concern knitting her brows. She dabbed the last remains of moisture from her eyes. "It isn't like you to hold a grudge."

"Grudge fudge!" Torie exclaimed with a defiant toss of her hair. "Dan Stewart *stole* my family home. I'm not about to forgive him."

"He did not steal it," Patty argued. "He bought it fair and square." She gave Torie a long, speculative look. "I know you're hurt, but let's keep things in perspective here. Legally he has as much right to that house as you do."

"Legally, maybe. Morally, he had none whatsoever."

"Oh dear," Patty murmured. "You're in worse shape than I ever dreamed. Maybe you'd better come inside so we can talk about this."

"I'd rather be alone."

"All the more reason not to be. Come on." She opened her door.

"But, Patty—"

"No buts. Either you come in willingly, or Jerry hauls you. Take your pick."

Torie glanced at Patty's husband, who had risen and now stood at the porch rail, waiting patiently for his wife. Since Torie knew he was perfectly capable of hauling her in and would do anything his sweetie asked of him, she wisely surrendered and opened her own door.

She would only stay long enough to appease Patty, and no matter what that old friend had to say, she would never, ever change her mind about Dan Stewart.

An hour later, Torie waved her goodbyes and got back into her car. In spite of herself, she felt better and grudgingly admitted that her talk with Patty really had helped her put the events of that day in their proper perspective. And while Torie might never forgive Dan for buying that beloved old house, she would most likely be able to speak civilly if she ever found herself face to face with him again.

Never mind that she would do everything in her power to assure that didn't happen in this lifetime.

As she did many evenings after a hectic day of teaching dance and aerobics in the little communities surrounding

England, Torie drove to her mother's café at the edge of town to talk with her parent and get a bite to eat. Erma Hanover, locally renowned for her culinary expertise, had purchased her eatery years ago with money she received from the sale of one hundred and fifty acres of farmland and the very house Dan Stewart now owned. Widowed when Torie was five, Erma hadn't had the manpower or expertise to run the massive farm alone. And though she'd sold everything and moved to town without complaint, Torie felt sure she had regrets.

Torie, herself, certainly did. Her life had changed drastically with the death of her father, and not for the better. Gone were lazy summer days full of sunshine, trains and picnics. Gone were the long winter nights filled with firelight, laughter and love. Her mother, trying to make a go of her newly opened café, labored from dawn until dusk seven days a week and left Torie in the care of her older brothers, twins of fifteen who resented a tagalong sis.

When Erma finally closed the café doors at night, she had little patience or energy left to devote to her rambunctious daughter. Feeling neglected, and sorely missing the doting dad who'd always had time for his precious "baby girl," Torie had longed to be back under the roof where she had been so sheltered, so secure, so satisfied.

As she grew to adulthood, she came to understand and even sympathize with her mother's problems as a single parent. This naturally resulted in a newfound closeness between mother and daughter.

Torie had even gone so far as to acknowledge that owning the old family home again probably *wouldn't* bring back the good old days. She never stopped dreaming of doing it, however, and faced now with the realization that she'd been cheated of what might be her only opportunity, she couldn't shake off her despondency. She dreaded telling her mother the news and could only hope she took it well.

On that thought, Torie looked at the digital clock on her car radio. She realized it was almost eight—closing time at Erma's Eatery. Her mom would be cleaning up the kitchen in a few minutes. Torie would help, as she often did, and make use of the opportunity to tell her mother what had happened. Though quite successful with her café these days, and able to hire all the help she needed, Erma still spent most of her time there. She loved visiting with all her regulars, and was a mother hen to old and young alike.

Torie spied the Eatery ahead and turned into the lot. In her distraction, she actually got out of her car before she noticed a very familiar truck and camper parked in a shadowy corner, several yards away from the utilitarian brick building. Her heart sank at the sight. Fairly certain that Dan wasn't in the beauty shop next door, and hoping he was in the Laundromat, she walked to the café and stepped inside.

A quick glance around the room revealed that Dan was not only there but sitting in a booth with Erma, who called out to Torie at once and waved her over. Lord, what a looker, Torie thought, her eyes riveted to Dan. She immediately banished that traitorous thought to regions unknown. Handsome or not, Dan was the enemy. And it was with dragging footsteps that she joined him and her mother at the table.

"Hi, sugar," Erma said, a greeting that warmed Torie's already flushed cheeks and put a smile on Dan's face.

"Hi," she replied, deliberately avoiding eye contact with him.

"Hungry?" her mother asked.

"A little."

"Then why don't I get you something to eat? You can sit here with Dan. He's anxious to talk to you, anyway."

So her mother already knew what had happened. Somehow that didn't surprise Torie nearly as much as the friendly smile Erma and Dan now exchanged. Miffed, Torie murmured, "I can get my own."

"No," Erma said. "You sit down." She slid out of the booth and perused Dan's plate, heaped with double portions of that day's special. "Can I get you anything, Dan?"

"Well...I could use another one of those wonderful biscuits," he replied with a grin that could charm the horns off a billy goat.

Though not a billy goat, much to Torie's disgust Erma reacted accordingly, blushing, laughing and disappearing into the kitchen. Disgusted, Torie eased into the booth and sat opposite Dan, who did not look up from his plate again or otherwise acknowledge her presence.

The silence between them grew awkward and Torie squirmed in her seat before her mother returned with her plate and a breadbasket brimming with her town-famous biscuits. Torie took the plate, all appetite gone now, and stared unenthusiastically at it.

"Now where were we?" Erma asked Dan as she nudged Torie over and sat down facing him.

"Uh...I was telling you about the first time I saw the house," Dan replied, reaching for a biscuit. He smiled slightly, a faraway look in his eye. "I'll never forget that day. It was summer. I had just spent my first long winter away from my dad—"

"Your parents are divorced?" Erma interjected.

"Yeah, when I was thirteen. Anyway, Dad and I were riding on the tourist train he engineered. We came round that big curve to the west of the house. We topped the rise, and there it was, everything I'd never have again . . ." His voice trailed to silence. He didn't move for a moment, then came to life with a soft laugh. "Sorry. That picture has haunted me for years. You can imagine how excited I was when I drove by the place this morning and saw that For Sale sign out front."

"I certainly can," Erma said with a solemn nod.

Torie could, too, and her heart twisted with renewed awareness of the immensity of her loss. So what, if he'd been speaking literally when he said he'd dreamed of that house since he was a kid. She'd dreamed of it, too. Suddenly irritated with her mother, who didn't seem the least interested in how *she* felt, Torie pushed her plate away.

"What's the matter?" the silver-haired woman asked, frowning. "Too much pepper on the potatoes?"

"The potatoes are perfect," Torie replied, adding, "May I see you in the kitchen for a moment?"

Erma gave her a motherly once-over and then nodded.

Torie led the way, plate in hand. Once there, she deposited it on the counter and turned on her parent. "Have you no shame? No loyalty?"

"Excuse me?" Erma arched an eyebrow.

"That man just bought our family home right out from under us."

"Family home? I believe you've forgotten that I only lived there six years, which was a fraction of the time I was married to Hal Hanover before he was killed. Why, I'd consider our place on Martin Road—the one your dad sold to buy the farm—more of a 'family home' than the house Dan bought today."

"Well, I wouldn't!" Torie exclaimed in frustration. "I was born in that house. I want to restore it, to live in it again, and I think it's disgraceful of you to fraternize with the man who stole it from me."

Erma stood in silence for a moment, solemn gray eyes on her agitated daughter. She sighed at what she saw and shook her head. "Have you been inside that house lately?"

"No," Torie admitted. "I was planning to meet Patty there this afternoon and take a walk through it so I could get an idea of what needed to be done to it. Unfortunately the new owner—" she grimaced "—was already there."

"That's a shame," Erma said. "I think such a walk-through would have been a real eye-opener for you. The house needs a lot of work inside, Torie. It's going to take a bundle of cold, hard cash to make it livable again."

"I make good money."

"And spend every cent of it on your car payment, your mobile-home payment and your studio rent. Add a mortgage to that, and you've got big problems."

"So I'll sell my mobile home. I won't be needing it once I get the house finished, anyway."

"And where do you plan on living in the meantime? Much as I love you, I'm not about to invite you into my tiny apartment. We'd kill each other before a week was out."

Torie could only agree with that sentiment, and crossing her arms over her chest, stared at her mother in thoughtful silence, momentarily stumped.

"I know you've clung to that restoration dream of yours for years," Erma continued, laying a comforting hand on Torie's shoulder. "And I know how hard it is to let go of it now. You must, however. The house belongs to someone else—a very nice someone else, who has the financial wherewithal to fix it up right. It's time to put that dream out of your mind, once and for all."

"How can I put it out of my mind?" Torie exclaimed, throwing her hands up in exasperation. "That roof was meant to shelter a family, those walls to echo laughter and love. Dan Stewart is a confirmed bachelor, a rolling stone who wants to modernize the place for a winter home. He'll ruin the house...and for what? He'll never be satisfied living in a town as small as England."

"Maybe so, maybe not. Time will tell. Right now he's a stranger and alone. If you can't accept him on a personal level, then do it on a professional one. As chairman of the City Council's greeting committee it's your duty to set aside your prejudices and make him feel welcome. England is desperate for new citizens, especially young, *eligible* ones."

"Eligible? Oh, for—" Torie sucked in a calming breath and counted to ten. Then she found room for her plate in the already packed dishwasher. "If you're thinking what I think you're thinking, you can just think again," she told her mother, who wasn't above matchmaking, if it would get her another one of those grandbabies she adored. "I would never, ever consider that man a possible. I want the Rock of Gibraltar like my dad. Dan is shifting sands, a man who lives on wheels three seasons out of the year and sits behind one during the other."

"Speaking of which," Erma interjected, handing Torie her glass, "won't it be exciting to have a celebrity living right here in England?"

"That's one word for it, I guess."

"I thought you liked racing. Lord knows, you went to enough races with your brothers, and I seem to recall that you idolized the drivers, even had a collection of autographs."

"I was an impressionable kid, then. As I said before, I appreciate another kind of man now, namely one with the desire to put down roots."

"But he's so sweet, so polite, so handsome."

"That's your opinion. Dan Stewart does not appeal to *me* in the least."

"Too bad. He's dying to get to know you better. Hopes the two of you can become friends."

"No, no and another no," Torie exclaimed in horror.

"'The lady doth protest too much, methinks.'"

"Mother!"

Acting as though she hadn't heard, Erma walked to the swing door, which opened into the dining room. She peeked out through the diamond-shaped window, then looked back at her daughter. "Leave those dishes. I'll finish up."

"I don't mind helping you."

"You don't have time tonight. Dan's going to follow you home. I told him there were vacancies in the trailer park where you lived."

"How could you do such a thing?" Torie blurted. "That park is so tiny I'll run into him every time I turn around."

"That did occur to me," Erma said with a sweet smile. "And I started not to say anything to Dan about it. But then I remembered all the times I've bragged about my daughter's ability to get along with anyone and decided this would be a wonderful chance for her to prove it. Chin up, sugar. It's time to forgive, forget and look to the future for a change."

Torie stood motionless for several moments after Erma left, the words *forgive* and *forget* ringing in her ears. Could she really do those things? she wondered, frowning. Could she?

And what about looking to the future?

Suddenly depressed at the thought of a future minus the house she'd planned on buying since childhood, Torie sagged against the counter. She didn't wallow in her self-pity long, however. Erma Hanover had issued a challenge, the same challenge Patty had issued barely an hour before. In her heart of hearts, Torie knew that they loved her and would never steer her wrong. She also knew she would never be able to look either of them—or herself—in the eye again if she didn't at least make an effort to do as they asked.

Muttering her disgust with life, in general, and auto racers, in particular, Torie deposited her glass in the dishwasher, squared her shoulders and pushed her way through the swing door. She found Dan talking to her mother at the cash register, open wallet in hand. His eyes focused on hers the moment she entered the room.

Summoning up a skill resulting from years of working with the public, Torie managed a tight-lipped smile. The brilliant smile she received in return nearly knocked her off her feet. Gulping, hand to her suddenly fluttering stomach, Torie headed straight for the exit.

"I'll be waiting out front," she murmured before she disappeared outside.

Once they were alone, Dan turned to Erma, disappointed and frowning. "She's still upset, isn't she?"

"Yes," the woman replied as she took his money and rang up the sale. "But I think she'll come around, once she gets to know you and hears your plans for the house. She thinks you're going to modernize, which would, in her opinion, 'ruin' it." Erma handed him his change.

He pocketed the coins. "She thinks that?"

"I'm afraid so."

"But I just want to restore it—to put it back like it was twenty years ago."

"I realize that." She frowned thoughtfully. "You know what might make Torie feel better about this whole thing?"

"What?" he asked.

"Getting her involved. Oh, I don't mean in a big way. The house is yours, after all. But if you're really going to restore it, you'll need to make at least one walk-through with someone who's familiar with the place, someone who used to live in it."

"Torie?"

"Torie."

"But what if she refuses?"

"Then *I'll* help you."

Dan nodded. "Thanks, Erma. For a great idea and for the meal, which was wonderful, by the way."

"You're very welcome."

"Are you open every night?" He shrugged sheepishly. "I'm a lousy cook, myself."

"Every night till eight," she told him with a grin.

Dan grinned back, glad his troubled conscience had sent him Erma Hanover's way. Not only had he gotten a damned good dinner, he could now rest assured that dear woman didn't care a bit that he'd bought her old house. He could only hope that Erma was right and Torie would soon feel the same.

Frankly, Dan doubted it. Torie seemed a little obsessed with the house, to his way of thinking. Why, she acted as if generations of Hanovers had lived there, which, according to Erma, wasn't true. So why her intense desire to own the place? he wondered. And why this barely concealed animosity toward him? A little resentment was to be expected, but she was downright hostile.

Not for the first time that day, Dan regretted that he hadn't told the vivacious blonde the truth immediately when they met. That error in judgment was most likely the major cause of her bad feelings toward him, and as a result he was going to have a difficult time even getting Torie to listen while he explained himself. But explain he would, and with a little luck she'd come to realize that he never meant to hurt her or the house. His intentions toward that place were as honorable as hers. He would cherish it to his dying day.

The cool night air felt good to Dan as he headed toward his truck once he'd exited the café. A quick glance in the direction of Torie's car confirmed that she was waiting for him. With a wave he got into his vehicle, and seconds later he trailed her up Highway 321. Minutes after that, she turned into a lighted trailer park. After stopping her car next to the mobile home where she undoubtedly lived, she got out and walked back to where he'd halted his own vehicle.

"Jack Porter owns the park," she told Dan as he stepped out onto the rocky ground. "He lives in that trailer there."

"Thanks."

She shrugged, turned and began walking away.

"Uh, Torie?"

She paused, not looking back.

"Do you have a few minutes? I'd like to talk to you."

"You'd better talk to Jack," Torie replied, half turning so that the beam from the security light overhead silhouetted her feminine curves and made her hair shimmer. "He goes to bed with the chickens and might not be too cooperative if you wake him."

"What about later, then...after I get hooked up?" Dan asked, drinking in the sight of those curves. His initial bad impression of her long vanished, he fervently wished they'd met under different circumstances. She was one sexy lady who could make his winters in England something to look forward to.

"We really have nothing to say to one another," Torie said, a reply that annihilated his half-formed fantasy of bearskin rugs and roaring fires under a roof they both loved. "Good night, Mr. Stewart."

"You may as well call me Dan," he stubbornly called to her retreating back. "We're going to be neighbors, after all, and maybe even friends."

Gritting her teeth at the very thought, Torie did not reply. Instead, she climbed her front steps, unlocked the door and escaped inside. She collapsed facedown on the daybed, which served as a couch, and covered her head with a throw pillow.

So much for accepting challenges. Apparently she wasn't up to this particular one. Twice, Dan had asked to talk with her. Twice, she'd refused him. Was that forgiving? Was that forgetting? Was that getting on with the future? Of course not.

Torie punched the pillow with her fist, then threw it at the door. Damn him. Damn Dan Stewart. Why had he come along and wrecked her life? And how would she ever get over it?

She got to her feet and scooped up a stack of dog-eared home-and-garden magazines, the ones she'd saved for years and pored over at length. Heartsick, she dropped them into the trash can. She wouldn't be needing them now. There wasn't much redecorating one could do to a tiny mobile home.

She walked to the corkboard mounted on the wall next to the telephone and took down a sun-faded photo. She started to toss it into the trash, but snatched it back at the last minute and, brushing it off, laid it gently between the pages of a picture album—an album full of similar family photos, most of which were set against a beautiful yellow house.

Sitting back down, Torie lay the open album across her lap and took a walk down memory lane. She smiled softly as she turned pages and gazed upon the photos. Her dad smiled back at her from many of them, a smile that brought to mind her very happy childhood.

How she'd loved him; how she loved him still. He would always have a place in her heart and in the hearts of everyone who knew him—family and friends alike. Hal Hanover had been a generous man, without prejudice and always willing to give anyone the benefit of the doubt. Erma Hanover was just like him, as were Torie's two brothers, Richard and Mack. Torie had always thought she was, too, but now she wondered.

Surely if she had inherited one tiny bit of her father's loving nature she would be able to accept what Dan Stewart had done and forgive him. As Patty pointed out, he had a legal right to purchase the house. Common sense told Torie he couldn't have known she existed, much less that she wanted the house so badly. She had no logical reason to blame him and should, maybe even *could* forgive.

Feeling somewhat better at that realization, Torie next looked to forgetting what he'd done. That would be much harder to do, of course. Every time she passed the house she would ache anew with the realization of what she'd lost. Dan would modernize, she would hate what he did.... Or would she? As her mom pointed out, he had the wherewithal to do a wonderful job of renovation. Maybe he'd surprise her. Maybe she'd even like what he did. Maybe forgetting wasn't going to be as bad as she thought.

Or maybe he'd decide he'd bitten off more than he could chew and sell it to her!

Torie smiled at the reappearance of her eternal optimism—the same optimism that had kept her hoping for the house all those years. Somewhat encouraged, she turned her thoughts to looking to the future. Well, two out of three isn't bad, she immediately decided, optimism back on the lam.

Ever since her teens, Torie had wanted nothing more than to marry a good man and raise a houseful of kids—an old-fashioned dream in a modern-day world. Only at the insistence of her mother, who'd learned about life after marriage the hard way, had Torie obtained a degree in the performing arts, ensuring that she would always be able to support herself as a dance teacher.

A year—and no husband—after graduation, Torie willingly acknowledged that she'd done the smart thing in pursuing a career. Even so, she would have traded said career in a New York minute for a man willing to sweep her off the dance floor and into her dream house.

Her dream house? Not exactly, and probably not ever.

Shaking her head ruefully, Torie refused to think any further about what would most likely be a remarkably uneventful future, if Dan didn't change his mind about the house. She'd forgiven and would try to forget. Surely that was enough to do her dad's memory proud.

Mentally patting herself on the back, Torie closed the album and put it away. Then, after walking to the window, she peeked out to find Dan busy unhooking the RV from his truck. Without hesitation, Torie opened her door and headed his way. Leveling and scotching a camper were jobs more easily handled by two and something she had done on camping trips with her brother Mack and his family. Maybe if she offered to help Dan, he would take that action as the apology she intended it to be and forget about that talk he said he wanted to have with her.

Torie certainly hoped so. Though she'd made great strides toward tolerating Dan Stewart in the past few minutes, she wasn't at all sure she was ready for a heart-to-heart with him, much less the friendship he'd mentioned.

Chapter Three

Dan, who'd shed his jacket and rolled his shirtsleeves to just below the elbow, didn't look up as Torie approached. Since the muddy gravel crunching underfoot had certainly heralded her arrival, she decided he must be ignoring her, and almost lost her nerve.

Almost.

Chewing her bottom lip, Torie bravely stood her ground not three feet away from where he knelt beside his RV, fiddling with something underneath it. The muscles of his massive forearms rippled with every move, fascinating Torie, who watched in appreciative silence for a long moment before she noisily cleared her throat.

Dan kept right on working.

"Need some help?" she finally asked.

He jumped as if he'd been shot, glanced over his shoulder at her, then laughed, obviously embarrassed. "Didn't hear you come up. Yeah, I could use a hand. I've only had this particular rig a month and I'm not really familiar with its hookup routine yet."

Though unfamiliar with this type of trailer herself, Torie nonetheless pitched in, applying what limited knowledge she did have. As always, two heads were better than one, and before long the ultramodern trailer was leveled and linked to electricity and water.

"Perfect," he said, grinning his pleasure when he reached inside to try the light switch and found it working. "Now how about a cold drink? I've got an ice chest full in the back of the truck."

"Thanks," Torie replied.

A moment later Dan handed her the cola she requested, opting for a root beer himself. They sat together on the lowered tailgate of the truck, where he touched the icy can to his brow, sweat-beaded in spite of the cool night. "I seem to recall that the man who sold me this thing said hookup was so simple a baby could do it."

"A baby Einstein, maybe," Torie murmured dryly, taking a refreshing swallow of her drink.

Dan laughed softly and did the same, then blotted his mouth and his forehead on the sleeve of his shirt. "You'd be a handy person to have around on a camping trip," he commented. "Been much?"

Before Torie could reply, Dan thumped at some mud on his jeans, a move that drew her gaze to his hands, blunt-tipped and masculine. Suddenly besieged with a vision of a double-width sleeping bag, a crackling fire and those same skillful hands on her body, a shocked-speechless Torie barely managed a reply. "Um, a time or two with my brother."

"Where do you usually go?"

"The mountains," she answered, oh, so casually, edging over to put precious inches between them so he wouldn't hear her thundering heart. "I, uh, especially love the Appalachians."

"Me, too," Dan said with an enthusiastic nod. He took another mouthful of his drink. "I've camped quite a lot, myself—of necessity, when I'm on the road, and for fun when I'm on vacation. I never get tired of waking up to a new view."

Torie, who wasn't in the least surprised by that, sipped her cola instead of asking why he'd just wasted his money on a home he would seldom occupy. She knew instinctively that his answer would most likely anger her, thereby shattering their fragile peace. For some reason, Torie didn't want to take that risk.

Dan, clearly unaware of her inner turmoil, said nothing else for a moment, then chuckled. "Speaking of such reminds me of the first time I camped. Was that ever a 'new view.' I'd just turned sixteen. Me and a couple of friends decided to celebrate by roughing it. You do understand what I mean by roughing it, don't you? Backpacks, fishing line, canteens. We didn't even take a tent. Wanted to sleep under the stars." He chuckled again.

In spite of herself, Torie smiled. She had no difficulty picturing a younger Dan and his two friends trekking to the woods. And having once tackled nature with the same confidence herself, she could presume what had happened.

"We started out okay," Dan continued. "The sky was blue, the air crisp, our energy level high. At noon we stopped at a lake, intending to angle for our lunch."

"Don't tell me, let me guess," Torie interjected. "You wound up eating chocolate bars, right?"

"Peanut butter, actually," Dan solemnly corrected her. "By that night, our mouths really watered for fresh trout.

We didn't have any better luck then, either, and it was peanut butter again."

Torie wrinkled her nose.

Dan grinned and continued. "Though all of us were ready to go back home by the next day, no one would admit it. So we forged ahead, sure we'd do better soon."

"But you didn't."

"No, we didn't, and as a result, ate peanut butter for lunch and then dinner again that day, too."

"It's a good thing you liked peanut butter," Torie commented.

"'Liked' being the key word here," Dan replied. "To this day I can't even smell the stuff without getting sick to my stomach."

She had to laugh. "So what happened?"

"Three days after we went up that mountain, we came down it—dirty, tired and several pounds lighter. I know, for a fact, that neither of those two guys who were with me have been camping since. Fortunately my dad took me again shortly after that—this time with proper gear and supplies. We had a great time, and I've loved the outdoors ever since."

"You were lucky to get a second chance."

"In many ways. My dad died two months after that trip. Thank God I have that memory."

They shared a smile of understanding then, a smile that touched Torie's heart and made her feel very close to this man who obviously loved the mountains, the trees and his dad as much as she did. No city slicker, Dan Stewart, she realized. The knowledge rattled Torie, since it attacked one of her prejudices against him.

At once, friendship didn't seem so out of the question. Confused, feeling a traitor to her dreams, Torie jumped abruptly to the ground. "I'm sorry, I just can't do this."

Clearly baffled, Dan leaped to the ground and blocked her path. "Do what?" he demanded, laying a hand on her shoulder.

"Be friends with you."

"But we were getting along so well. Was it something I said?"

Intensely aware of his proximity, Torie barely heard the question. Her skin tingled where Dan touched it. Her pulse raced in response to his searching gaze, which lingered on her mouth. If she hadn't known better, she'd have sworn he wanted to kiss her. Worse, she'd have sworn she wanted to kiss him back.

Damn, Torie thought, breathless with anticipation at the very thought. Forgiving and forgetting the man was one thing, she ruefully acknowledged. Lusting after him, quite another. Disgusted with herself, she purposefully resurrected all her earlier feelings of resentment and anger, feelings that had almost died a natural death.

"Not something you said," she exclaimed. "Something you did. That house should be mine, Dan Stewart, and I cannot, will not forgive you for taking it from me." Whirling, Torie jogged to her trailer.

"Well, hell," Dan muttered, watching until she disappeared indoors. He crushed the can in his hand to vent some of his frustration, then tossed it into a nearby trash can, where it clattered its way to the bottom. Wincing at the sound, Dan glanced quickly at Jack Porter's trailer. He'd already woken that grouchy old man once already this night, and he didn't want to do it again.

Shoulders slumped, spirits flagging, Dan lifted the ice chest out of his truck and walked to his trailer. He stepped up into it, a second later depositing his load with a dull thump on the table. Flipping open the lid, Dan reached for another drink, then thought better of it. Another root beer would do nothing for his bad mood. A smile from Torie would do wonders, however. And a kiss...well, there was just no telling what one of those might accomplish.

Now where did that come from? Dan stood in thoughtful silence for a moment trying to think of a single reason for this and all the other lustful thoughts that had danced in his head the whole time he and Torie worked on the trailer. He came up with several good reasons right away, not the least of which were her striking good looks.

Dan dropped down on the couch, which made into a bed at night, and rubbed his tired eyes. Though concerned about Torie and feeling somewhat like the villain in a Saturday-morning serial, he really had no intentions of getting involved with her on any level other than friendship. So what if her body drove him wild? So what if he'd die for one taste of those pouty lips of hers? He was surely adult enough to handle a simple sexual attraction, even one as unwanted, unexpected and unprecedented as this one was. Besides, Torie didn't share the attraction. At least he didn't think so. There were a couple of times in the past hour when he'd actually thought...

But, no. Nothing had changed between them, and once he alleviated his guilt feelings by talking to Torie, he would find out what he needed to know about his new property and exit her life as abruptly as he'd entered it. He'd restore the house, move into it with a clear conscience and then, if he was still lonely, find himself a housemate.

A four-legged housemate, that is. God knows, a man always knew where he stood with a dog.

Dan rose the next morning actually a bit more weary than when he had retired. Sleep had eluded him, and the victory he'd experienced upon finding and buying the house was decidedly hollow now. He realized it probably would be until he made his peace with Torie.

Since a quick glance out the window revealed that she was not home, Dan gulped down his usual breakfast of coffee and chocolate-chip cookies and headed straight for Erma's Eatery. He had no idea where Torie worked but figured Erma could tell him.

After greeting him warmly, Erma did just that, directing him to Torie's dance studio, which was in back of the same building that housed the café. Dan, who hadn't even known Torie was a dance instructor and was quite curious about the lively music blaring through the thin walls, headed that way immediately.

Walking around the side of the building, Dan marveled that a town the size of England could support a dance studio. He decided that Torie must surely have another means of support, then remembered the leotard she had on the day before. It seemed as though she taught dance two days a week, anyway.

Dan opened the door with some hesitation and then entered the studio, which appeared to be a converted storage area. After a quick perusal of the place, he took a seat on one of the folding chairs at the back of the room, joining a handful of other observers, most likely parents. At the front of the room, the walls of which were lined with mirrors and a dance barre, stood five little girls, who looked to be preschoolers.

Dan had never seen so many ribbons and ruffles in his life, and grinned at the sight. That grin froze and faded when his eye fell on Torie, who'd appeared from nowhere and was now walking toward the dancers, her tap shoes clicking with every step. Dressed in shimmering blue tights and a canary yellow leotard that hugged and enhanced every breathtaking curve, she was a sight to behold.

He watched, enthralled, while she worked with the children, a task that involved showing them slow-motion dance steps to the accompaniment of a song he vaguely remembered from his youth, "The Tennessee Wig Walk." Every time the words *wig walk* emanated from the speakers of the cassette deck sitting on the floor nearby, all the dancers wiggled their cute little behinds.

While this was adorable on a three- or maybe four-year-old, it was sexy as hell on a twenty-plus-year-old. Dan found he could barely breathe, so affected was he by the sight of Torie twisting and jiggling to the music. Squirming to ease the sudden snugness of his jeans, Dan glanced at the other members of the audience, none of whom appeared as agitated as he.

Though that realization only served to disconcert him further, he still couldn't drag his eyes away from her. By the time the dance ended, Dan was wired. Tense, flustered, he suddenly decided that talking to Torie might not be such a good idea, after all, and stood to make his exit. But it was too late. She'd already seen him.

Gulping audibly, Dan got a quick grip on his scattered wits, if not his libido. He mustered a smile and waved. She nodded slightly in response, pushed back a strand of hair that had escaped from her ponytail, then turned her back on him to talk to a parent. Challenged by her obvious lack of enthusiasm—and perhaps a little insulted—Dan waited until Torie was alone. Then he joined her, carefully keeping his gaze above her chin and his hands behind his back.

"Hi," he said, suddenly as gawky as a teenager on his first date. At once, Dan wished he'd never stepped through her studio door. In his present addled state, he was bound to do or say something he'd regret.

"Hi."

"Uh, nice place you have here." *Brilliant lead-in, Danny Boy. Brilliant.* Dan's face began to burn.

"It serves its purpose." Torie took off her hair clip and shook out her burnished gold curls, demolishing the scant remains of his composure. Bending over, she dug a brush from her nearby carryall and without straightening began to use it.

"Are you finished for the day?" *At ten in the morning? Yeah, right.* Dan gave himself a mental kick in the pants.

Torie straightened and began to brush back her hair. Skillfully she refastened the clip, capturing all the feathery strands that had escaped while she danced. "No. I have classes until six this evening."

"I see. Do you stop for lunch?" *No, she eats while she taps.* Dan retrieved a handkerchief from his back pocket and nervously dabbed at the sweat snaking down his neck. "I still need to talk to you . . . to explain—"

"Look, Dan," Torie interjected, tossing the brush back into the bag. "You don't owe me an explanation of any kind. The house is yours, now. You can do whatever you want to it."

"But all I want to do is put it back like it was when I first saw it."

She caught her breath. "You mean you're not going to rip out the walls, carpet the hardwood floor or lower the ceilings?"

"Where in the hell did you get an idea like that? I'm going to *restore* the house and I was kind of hoping you'd act as consultant. You did live in it at one time."

Torie's eyes narrowed. She tilted her head, frowning thoughtfully at him. "Is that why you came by today? To ask for my help?"

"Yes, and to apologize," Dan blurted.

"Apologize?" Clearly she was as surprised by that announcement as Dan was.

Cursing his addled wits, he tried to salvage the situation. "Yeah. I'm, um, really sorry things turned out this way."

"Sorry enough to sell the house to me? You could make a few bucks on it and build yourself another one...far, far away."

That sobered Dan, who bristled at her proposal. Never in his life had he met a more stubborn woman, and he rued the apology he hadn't intended to make in the first place. "I may be sorry, but I'm not *that* sorry. Now, I'm leaving for Charlotte early on Saturday and I'd like to get some repairs lined up before I go. Are you going to help me or not?"

"Not!" she exclaimed. They glared at each other a moment, both fuming and ready to do battle.

"Torie?" She turned at the sound of her name and found the mother of one of her students right behind her. "Do you have a spare second? I have some questions about Julie Beth's recital costume."

"Of course," Torie replied, whirling and leading her away. Out of the corner of her eye, she saw Dan pivot and stride from the room, slamming the door behind him. Ten minutes after he left, Julie Beth's mother left, too, leaving Torie alone in the vast room.

Troubled, ashamed of herself for the near argument with Dan, Torie set to work preparing for the next class, less than thirty minutes away. She rewound the audiotape and stored it, then located new music. That accomplished, Torie slipped out of her tap shoes and into a pair of sneakers. Scooping up her purse, she snatched up her ever-handy wraparound skirt and headed for the door, brunch on her mind. Having missed dinner the night before and breakfast that morning, she was starved.

Erma looked up and waved as Torie entered the café, legs modestly covered by the skirt. Opting not to tie up a table, Torie made her way to the counter instead, where she seated herself on one of the swivel stools.

"What'll you have?" her mom asked.

"Coffee and a doughnut, I think."

Her mom filled two cups of coffee, put a chocolate-glazed doughnut on a plate and joined her daughter at the counter.

"Feeling better today?"

"So-so," Torie hedged, too ashamed of her blue mood to be more specific.

"Was that Dan I saw getting into his truck a few minutes ago?"

"Probably. He came by the studio to see me."

"Oh? What did he have to say?"

"He told me he was going to restore the house instead of modernizing it and asked me to act as a sort of consultant."

"That's a marvelous idea!"

Suddenly suspecting where Dan might have gotten that "marvelous idea," Torie glared at her mother. "Did you put him up to it?"

"I merely suggested that he walk through the place with someone who could tell him what used to be where. He thought of you all on his own."

"Oh, Mother," Torie moaned, putting her fingers to her temples and pressing at the sudden pain there.

"It'll be good for you. I'm sure that once you see how much work such a restoration involves, you'll—"

"I'm not going to do it."

"What?"

"I told him, 'no.'"

"Torie, Torie," Erma scolded. "What am I going to do with you?"

"Nothing. I'm a lost cause."

Erma lay an arm across her shoulder, hugging her hard. "You're not a lost cause."

"Then why can't I do the adult thing and be friends with that man?"

"You can and you will . . . in time. Don't rush it." Erma sighed. "Poor thing. I guess I haven't seemed very sympathetic to your problems, have I?"

Torie shrugged.

"Well, if I haven't, it's for a reason. You've been obsessed with that house ever since I sold it. Though I'm not sure why, I have my suspicions, and I'm here to tell you that you cannot recreate what can never be again."

"Well, you can't recreate what never was, either," Torie retorted. "And you and I both know that's what Dan is trying to do."

Erma shook her head, sighing heavily. "What either of you sees in that old place is beyond me. Why, it was damp, dark, hot in summer and cold in winter. I was thrilled to get rid of it."

Torie, now nibbling on her doughnut, couldn't believe her ears and wondered fleetingly if she'd lost her perspective through the years. No, she immediately decided. The house had been every bit as wonderful as she remembered, and it could be so once again. She still wanted it—always would.

The jingle of the bell on the door heralded the arrival of a customer and broke into her thoughts. Torie glanced at her watch, exclaiming her dismay when she saw the time.

"I've got to run," she said, leaping from the stool and digging into her purse for a dollar bill, which she lay on the counter. "Are you going to the Council meeting tonight?"

"Yes," her mom replied with a nod.

"I'll pick you up," Torie said. She started for the door, but whirled to run back and kiss her parent on the cheek. "I do love you, Mom."

"Ah lub oo doo," her startled mother replied around a mouthful of the doughnut Torie had abandoned.

Laughing, spirits almost back to normal, Torie ran out the door and into the sunshine of an autumn Tennessee day.

Torie clung to her good mood through the rest of the day and on into the meeting, quite an accomplishment since the town's newest citizen was naturally the topic of conversation and of business.

Surprising no one, Susan Winters, also on the Council, volunteered to act as a one-woman welcome committee, escorting Dan around the countryside, introducing him to everyone, showing him the ropes of rural living. Susan, unhappily married to an oft-absent trucker, was always on the prowl for a good time—one of the reasons she and Torie did not get along. Barely two months before, Susan had made a play for Torie's brother, Richard, who had been home for a visit without his wife of seven years. Though Richard was not tempted and claimed to find the situation highly amusing, Torie was livid and quite vocal about it. As a result, she and Susan barely tolerated each other.

Tonight, however, Torie actually found herself on Susan's side. As chairman of the greeting committee, welcoming duties naturally fell to Torie. If Susan took on those duties, Torie could avoid Dan with a clear conscience. Smiling to herself at the very thought, Torie opened her mouth to verbalize her support of the brunette's plan.

"I hope the view from Susan's bedroom is nice," Erma murmured, sotto voce, before Torie could utter a word. "That's probably all of England the two of them will ever see . . . at least while they're together."

Assailed by a vision of Susan and Dan not only together but in Susan's boudoir, Torie almost swallowed her tongue. Without further thought, she blurted, "I believe welcoming Dan is my responsibility."

"But you're so busy," Susan argued, smiling sweetly. "Why, you're in a different town every day of the week teaching those dance classes of yours. When will you find time to entertain Dan?"

"My weekends are free," Torie said, unable to resist adding, "And my nights."

Though Susan's smile never faded, her eyes bored holes through Torie. "How lucky for Dan that you're a spinster."

Only Erma's hand, clutching Torie's arm, kept her in her seat. "How lucky for Dan that you're not."

Erma sputtered with laughter at that, laughter that multiplied and soon filled the meeting room, situated at the rear of the newspaper office. Susan and Torie reluctantly joined in moments later, and it was on a much lighter note that the meeting continued.

It was business as usual for the rest of the night, but Torie paid little heed. Having opened her big mouth and volunteered to welcome Dan, she now tried to rationalize her actions. It hadn't been jealousy that prompted that impulsive offer, no sirree. It had been . . . um . . .

In desperation, Torie racked her brain for a motive and failing that, hatched a scheme so diabolically clever she couldn't believe she'd actually thought of it.

Dan Stewart claimed he intended to live to a ripe old age in England and from all appearances meant it. He had bought a house here, after all, and refused to sell it to her. But did he really know what he was getting into? Torie wondered.

She seriously doubted it. For all his experience in the out-of-doors, he hailed from Daytona. Most likely he had no idea what rural life entailed, in spite of her previous attempts to warn him. Looking back at those attempts, Torie decided that she'd been too obvious before, no doubt the reason Dan had not been receptive to her comments.

Why not make good use of the time she would spend welcoming him to England by *showing* instead of *telling* him the perils of small-town living? He would be around until Saturday. With that length of time at her disposal, she could be much more subtle.

Encouraged, Torie spent the rest of the meeting making a mental list of the bad things about living in the country. Never mind that she could have made a twice-as-long list of the good. She intended to accentuate only the negative in her campaign to discourage Dan from actually going through with the restoration of the house and settling in England. Torie decided that these negatives seemed to fall into two categories: physical inconveniences and social inconveniences. She resolved to deal with the physical first.

Eager to get on with her campaign, Torie bid her co-members a hasty goodbye when the meeting finally adjourned and after dropping her mother off at her car drove straight to Dan's place. She suspected he might not be thrilled to see her—especially in light of that morning's near skirmish—but vowed to choke down some humble pie and apologize if that was what it took to make amends. A woman with a plan, she was certain that if she played her cards right he would be more than ready to sell her the house come Friday. He could then leave England via the same highway that had brought him there, footloose again and none the worse for his experience.

Dan's truck was parked in front of his lighted trailer when she pulled into the drive, a sure indication that he was home. But when Torie knocked on the door, no one answered. With growing concern she waited what seemed an eternity, then knocked again, jumping nervously when the door suddenly opened. Torie, who had her welcome-to-England speech all prepared, forgot every word of it when she found her eyes even with the world-famous pecs Dan's shirts had heretofore hidden from view.

She recognized them this time and, weak-kneed, clutched the doorjamb to keep from landing in an undignified heap at his feet. Raising her gaze with difficulty, Torie noted the droplets of water on Dan's muscled shoulders and neck and his hair, tousled and curling damply around his handsome face. Obviously she'd dragged him from the shower.

Dragged him from the shower? Didn't she just wish!

Pulse racing at the very thought, Torie let her eyes drop to encompass Dan's flat belly, gray gym shorts and long legs. Lord, what a hunk, she thought, raising her gaze just in time for Dan's smile to finish her off.

"Hi, Torie," he murmured, obviously surprised and maybe even pleased.

Encouraged, she smiled back. "Hi, yourself. I wasn't sure you'd speak to me after the way I acted this afternoon."

"I wasn't exactly Prince Charming, myself," he murmured with a rueful laugh. "And it was totally unrealistic of me to think you'd agree to help restore the house. If I had it to do again, I'd never ask that of you."

"But you must. I'm looking forward to helping you."

His jaw dropped. "You are?"

"I am."

"Why, that's great!" he exclaimed. "Just great. I've been clearing rubble from the place all afternoon and I've got to tell you, I'm really excited about what I've found so far. Did you know that the banister is made of solid teakwood?"

Of course Torie knew, and sick at the thought that her children would never slide down that banister, she struggled to get a handle on her hyperactive hormones. She had a job to do. It was time to round up her scattered wits and keep a tight rein on them . . . if she could.

"Actually I didn't come here just to talk about the house," Torie said, sidestepping his question. "I came on business. As chairman of the City Council's greeting committee, it's my pleasure to officially welcome you to England."

"Oh, really?" Dan asked with obvious amusement.

"Uh-huh. And to volunteer my services as hostess, guide and whatever else it might take to make you feel at home."

"Thanks."

"Don't mention it. Now, I believe you told me that you're leaving town on Saturday."

"That's right. I have a race in Charlotte, North Carolina, next week and should really be there already."

"Then I'd like to throw a party for you on, say Friday night. I thought I'd invite some locals in your age group so you can meet and get to know them. How does that sound?"

"Perfect. I really appreciate it." Dan stood in silence for a moment, a thoughtful look on his face. "Does this mean you've forgiven me for buying the house, after all?"

"Oh, yes," Torie replied with complete honesty. She had . . . several times.

"And does it mean that we're friends?"

Friends? Torie realized with a start that she craved something much more physical than friendship with Dan Stewart. The knowledge distressed and frightened her. Torie, who'd been raised on traditional values, did not believe in sex before marriage. Dan Stewart with his mobile life-style was not, but *not* husband material in her eyes. Therefore the desire she felt for him was more than just a nuisance that threatened the effectiveness of her quest. It indicated a shocking lack of morals.

"Torie?" Dan's voice jerked her back to the present.

"Oh, uh, of course we're friends," she stammered, mentally vowing to ignore and hide her attraction to him. "Now, when would you like me to walk through the house with you?"

"How about tomorrow?" Dan said. "Do you have any time to spare? I'm free all day."

"Well, I teach at Rush tomorrow. That's only twenty minutes away, and I do have a long lunch break . . ." She paused, plotting her day. "If I met you shortly after ten, do you think we'd be able to take care of business in time for me to grab a bite to eat and be back there by twelve-thirty?"

"I'm sure of it."

"Then tomorrow it is." Torie gave him a smile. "And now that we've settled that, I think I'd better go on home. It's been a long day and I'm beat."

She turned to leave but was halted when Dan caught her hand and pulled her back. Thinking he had something else to say, Torie turned expectantly. To her astonishment he wrapped his other arm around her, pulling her closer.

"What are you doing?" she blurted, disconcerted at suddenly finding herself in the embrace of this man she found so appealing. She clutched his biceps with her free hand.

"Thanking you for your welcoming efforts so far," Dan replied quite solemnly. That said, he lowered his head and brushed his lips over hers in a kiss so brief it could only be considered chaste.

Yet Torie felt the shock of it clear to the bone. Stunned, she gaped at him. Her brain screamed caution; her tingling lips begged for more . . . much more . . . all he had to give. Bewildered by the scrambled signals, Torie clung to him in breathless indecision.

Dan had no such problems. Clearly as startled by the megacharge as Torie was, he tightened the embrace and kissed her again.

And what a kiss it was. Longer, harder, hotter, this one wasn't one bit chaste. Torie could have sworn she felt the earth jolt beneath her feet.

Or was it just her heart slamming into her rib cage?

As frightened by her wanton reaction as she was by his fever, Torie tipped her head back to break the searing contact. Dazed, chest heaving, she jerked her hand free of Dan's and wedged it between them.

"No!" she exclaimed, pushing with all her strength.

Clearly startled by her vehemence, Dan released her. Torie backed away from him, only to halt abruptly when her body met the solid obstacle of her car. Gratefully she sagged against it. Her troubled gaze found and locked with Dan's, and though sorely tempted to vent her embarrassment on him, Torie held her peace. That second kiss was as much her fault as Dan's, and she knew it.

"You okay?" He was frowning now, watching her anxiously.

Torie had no doubt he thought their newly formed friendship had just gone up in smoke. She blushed, knowing he had just cause, especially in light of her mercurial moods of late. How was he supposed to know she'd turned over a new leaf and would do anything—well, almost anything—to ensure that peace prevailed?

Taking a deep breath, Torie managed a smile intended to put his mind at ease. "I'm okay. I just need to get on home. I have a full day tomorrow—three dance classes, two senior citizens' aerobics sessions and a walk through an old house with a new friend."

"We're still on?" She heard his relief.

"Of course we are," Torie said. "And I'll see you then."

She allowed herself one last long look at this "new friend" who was every woman's fantasy, then deliberately turned her back on his charms. Tonight's experience had taught Torie much. Though not the sort of man a homebody such as herself should ever consider a possibility, Dan Stewart was nonetheless temptation with a capital everything. If she intended to charm him out of that house of his *and* hold onto her virtue, she would have to keep her distance.

She could only pray he would keep his, too.

Chapter Four

Lunch break on Wednesday rolled around too soon, and not soon enough. Torie, who'd had a definite problem concentrating on her young students' shuffle-step-steps and turn-two-three-fours that morning, was a nervous wreck by the time she headed her car out of Rush at ten o'clock to make the drive to England.

Part of Torie knew that she had to stand up and do battle for the house that was hers by right. Part of her wanted to let it go so she could run as far and as fast as necessary to get Dan Stewart out of her life and off her mind.

Torie knew the reason for these sudden second thoughts, of course: a simple thank-you kiss, which, when rated on a scale of "so-so" to "fine," earned a whopping "awesome!" And while such important questions as *Will today's walk-through be enough to discourage him?* and *Will I actually have to throw a party?* should have been first and foremost in her mind, all she really wanted to know was *Will he kiss me again?*

For that reason, Torie lectured herself all the way to her destination. And for that reason, her heart did a back flip when her eager eyes spotted Dan waiting by his truck, every bit as dashing—and irresistible—as the first time she saw him.

Torie greeted him with remarkable calm, considering the shaky state of her nerves and morals. Dan, on the other hand, was clearly wired and impatient to get on with the tour. Taking her hand, he practically dragged her into the house.

"I've been cleaning ever since I got here early this morning," he said with a smile of pride, when they had shut the door behind them. "Tell me you're impressed."

"I'm impressed," Torie dutifully responded. In actuality, *shocked* would better have described her state of mind. The living room, which she'd always considered huge, as a youngster, looked tiny to her twenty-two-year-old eyes. And what a mess it was. The ceiling, stained and cracked, sagged in one corner. The walls, flaking and peeling onto varnish-bare wooden floors, displayed a mélange of colors, courtesy of the various renters who had lived there.

Dismayed, Torie pirouetted slowly, taking note of every nook and cranny of this room where she'd spent so many happy hours. She ended her inspection at the fireplace and sighed her relief when she realized time had not altered her memory of it, at least. From mantel to hearth, it looked exactly the same as it had seventeen years ago. She could almost see her dad on one knee in front of it, carefully arranging the logs for maximum burning time.

"Torie?"

Lost in her memories, Torie couldn't be totally sure she'd actually heard Dan calling. She shook her head to clear it, realized she was alone, and hurried to the source of the sound, most likely the hall.

"Did you call?" she asked, when she found Dan there.

"Yeah," he said, with a frown adding, "Is something wrong?"

"No," she lied, flustered by the question. Was her emotional state so easy to read? Would her less-than-honorable motives be equally transparent?

Dan hesitated, then shrugged. Motioning for her to follow, he led the way down the narrow hallway, which Torie knew led to the master bedroom. They peered into the room through the doorway.

"Was this walk-in closet here when you lived in the house?" he asked, pointing to what was obviously a modern-day addition.

"Yes," Torie told him. "My dad built it when he and mother moved in."

"He did a good job. What about that pantry in the kitchen?" Dan next asked, striding back down the hall before she could reply. Torie hid her smile at his excitement. It was a wonder he didn't leave a vapor trail behind him. He was certainly moving at jet speed.

"I think it was there when they bought the house," she called after him, not following. "You'd better ask Mom to be sure." Making use of the time alone, Torie walked on into the bedroom to make closer inspection. Much smaller than she remembered, this room, too, sported peeling paint and stained ceilings.

Torie shook her head in disbelief at the changes time and a handful of renters had wrought on her beloved house. Erma was right. It would take a small fortune—or maybe even a large one—to restore the house to its former glory. Why, it would almost be simpler to just tear the place down and . . .

Tear the place down! Horrified at the very thought, Torie spun on her heel and collided with Dan, who'd most likely come looking for her.

"There you are," he said, setting her back on her feet without ceremony. "Come with me to the porch. I have a question to ask about it."

"Which is?"

"Was it always screened-in?"

"For as long as I can remember," Torie replied. "We spent a lot of time on the swing out there and needed the screen to keep the mosquitoes away."

"Good. Now about the living room—"

Living room? He was back in there? Torie did smile then, and Dan saw it.

"What's so funny?" he asked.

"You are," she told him with a chuckle. "Why, you're practically bouncing off the walls."

"I guess I am," Dan admitted with a sheepish grin. "But we only have a little while to do this and I have a lot of questions."

"Then why don't we organize? Take it a room at a time?" Torie suggested. "We'll start in the living room and work our way upstairs."

"Great idea," Dan exclaimed, laying an arm across her shoulders and firmly propelling her in that direction. Once there, he released her and began to pace, further evidence of his agitated state. Torie crossed her arms over her chest, watching with envy and maybe a little resentment. But for a quirk of fate, she would be the excited one, the one with the big plans.

That realization sobered her. Mission reaffirmed, she set to the task at hand—talking Dan Stewart out of his house. "The ceiling and walls are a mess, aren't they?"

"Nothing a good drywall man can't set to rights."

"Are you going to replace the floor? It has some really worn spots."

"I think a new board here and there will do the trick—and a fresh varnish job, of course."

"Of course." Torie walked to the stairs and played her fingers over the spindles supporting the teak banister of which Dan was so proud. Deliberately she turned to him. "The steps are quite steep. That could prove a problem if you plan on having little ones around some day."

"You know I don't," he told her.

Torie nodded and shifted her gaze back to the stairs. "I remember the time my brother Mack fell down these. He would take them at a run, no matter how many times my mother got after him. Anyway, he tripped here—" she raised on tiptoe to touch a step way over her head "—and tumbled all the way down. Knocked out one of his front teeth. He was thirteen at the time, so it was a permanent one. Mom drove like a maniac to get him to the nearest dentist fifty miles north."

"Is the dentist still that far away?"

"No, only about thirty miles these days," Torie said, pleased Dan had not missed the point of her story. "Now what do you want to know about this room?"

He told her, and it was nearly twenty minutes later before the two of them moved on to the kitchen. Torie glanced at her watch.

"We'd better step things up. It's already eleven and if I'm going to allow myself time to eat, I need to pull away from here by eleven-thirty at the latest."

"Right, right," Dan said. Words tumbling out of his mouth, he asked questions about the water system, the gas lines and flooring. Torie answered what she could, liberally sprinkling each response with a negative memory calculated to give Dan second thoughts about his purchase. She described the problems encountered with electricity that went off at the drop of a hat, thereby shutting down the pump that supplied indoor water. She expounded eloquently regarding the outdoor propane tank, which supplied the stove and always seemed to need filling on Saturday, when no deliveries were made.

Dan nodded solemnly in response and then headed upstairs, apparently undaunted. Unsure of her progress with him, Torie trailed a little more slowly.

As always, the view from the windows in those two bedrooms was breathtaking. Just visible in the distance to the south were the mountains, rugged and majestic, and to the east, pastureland, patchworked fields and a white frame church with a tall steeple.

The beauty was not lost on Dan, who heaved a sigh. "I've been a lot of places in my life, but this is surely one of, if not *the* prettiest."

"It is, isn't it?" Torie murmured. She walked to a southern window and looked out at the road. "And I've always loved it. Unfortunately it didn't look so wonderful to my brothers, who had to stand out in the rain, sleet and snow waiting on the school bus. They rode on that bus three hours every day."

"Three hours!"

"That's right. Got on it at seven in the morning, got off it at five."

"My God, that's deplorable."

"But necessary. England had an enormous bus route, involving many unpaved rural roads."

"I gather some of the neighboring towns sent their children to England's schools?"

"Still do." She smiled. "But what do you care? You aren't going to have any kids to ride the bus, anyway."

"True," he said. He glanced around the room. "I haven't seen a telephone jack anywhere but in the kitchen. I'd have thought some of the renters would have had an extension up here, even if your family didn't."

"My dad hated the phone and used it only when necessary. That's just as well, I guess. We shared a party line with five other families and probably couldn't have used it when we wanted to, anyway."

"Five other families?" She heard his gulp.

"That was years ago, of course. You probably won't have more than a couple on yours."

"You mean I won't be able to get a private line?"

"There's always that chance," Torie said, hiding her glee at his obvious distress behind what she hoped was a sympathetic smile.

The smile was fine. It was the twinkle in her eyes that gave her away. Dan saw it and bit back a smile of his own, suddenly reassured about his impulsive decision to buy the house. So Torie was trying to pull a fast one, eh? Trying to turn him against rural living? To his way of thinking that just proved he'd made the right decision, after all.

Why else would she go to so much trouble to convince him otherwise? She obviously thought he would change his mind about the place and put it back on the market. Then, no doubt, she would snatch it right up, flaws and all. Well, he had no intention of falling for her little scheme, and the sooner she realized it, the better off she would be.

Not that Dan wanted her to give up her quest any time soon. Lord knows, he didn't. In truth, he found Torie's efforts to change his mind quite entertaining, and couldn't help but wonder just how far she would go to convince him to sell the house. Tantalized by that thought—and the memory of that shocker of a kiss they'd shared the night before—Dan vowed to find out.

"So what are your bedroom questions?" Torie asked, breaking into his thoughts.

Dan nearly swallowed his tongue. Not daring to verbalize the "bedroom question" first and foremost on his mind, he proceeded instead to ask Torie about upstairs closets and the bathroom situated between the two rooms.

"I guess that's all I need to know for now," he commented, after she explained how her dad utilized parts of both sleeping areas to provide space for the bath.

"What about the attic?" Torie asked.

"There's an attic?" He hadn't realized that.

"Uh-huh," she told him. With brisk steps, she led the way out into the hall, where she halted, flipped on a light and looked up at the ceiling.

Dan's gaze followed hers and found what he recognized as a cover for disappearing folding steps. He noted the short length of the pull chain suspended from it.

"Oh, dear," Torie murmured. "The chain is broken. We'll never be able to reach it without a ladder."

"Maybe if I give you a boost?" Dan stepped behind Torie and placed his hands on her waist before she could object. With a muttered "Ready?" he lifted her up to where she could grasp the chain, which promptly slipped out of her hand when he lowered her. "Wrap it around your fingers," he prompted, laying his hands on her tiny waist once more. "Again now, ready?"

This time Torie was better prepared, and with her cooperation, Dan was able to lift her high enough for her to loop the chain a couple of times before she tugged on it. With a groan worthy of a horror movie, the cover gave way and lowered on its hinge, revealing the tri-folded steps and several cobwebs.

Releasing Torie rather reluctantly—it felt mighty nice to have her cute little tush so near his jackhammering heart—

Dan reached up to extend the ladder to the floor. "Ladies first," he said.

"No thanks," Torie replied, eyeing the dangling cobwebs with obvious distaste.

Chuckling, Dan climbed the ladderlike steps.

To his surprise, he found not the rafter-exposed storage area he'd expected but a small room, complete with hardwood floors, paneled walls and an octagon-shaped window.

Dan couldn't believe his eyes and turned slowly so he wouldn't miss one lovely detail of the area, which, if the shelves lining the north wall were anything to go by, had once been a study or maybe an office.

"It looks just like it always did," Torie exclaimed with obvious delight from her vantage point partway up the steps. Hurriedly she climbed the rest, joining him in the middle of the room.

"An office?"

"Yes," Torie said. "My dad's hideout. He kept all his farming records up here, as well as his favorite books." She walked to the shelves and closed her eyes, clearly caught up in a pleasant memory. "They were stacked in here two deep—everything from Shakespeare to Erle Stanley Gardner. He loved them all."

"Tell me about your dad," Dan said, hoping for insight into Torie's fixation on the house. Something—maybe a sixth sense he had where fathers were concerned—told him her obsession might have something to do with her relationship with that parent. Dan acknowledged that wasn't so unreasonable. His own deep feelings for the place were certainly influenced by a loving father-child relationship.

Dropping down on the edge of the entrance to the room, legs dangling over the hallway below, Dan patted the floor next to him in invitation. Torie hesitated, then joined him.

"My dad was a wonderful man," she said, once she was seated a good six inches away. "Everyone loved him. You would have, too."

"I believe you said he was a farmer?"

"Not always, but that's what he did the whole time I knew him."

"What did he do for a living before that?" Dan asked.

"He owned a café, actually the same one Mom owns now. Dad sold it and their house in town to buy this farm."

"You said he died when you were five?"

Torie sighed. "Yeah. He was only fifty and had been farming six years at the time. It was a tractor accident that should never have happened."

"God, I'm sorry."

She blinked rapidly and looked away, visibly moved. "Mom tried to hire on some help and keep up the place, but it was just too much for her. I don't think she would have given up if my brothers had shown the least interest in farming. But they both told her flat out that they wanted no part of slaving from sunup until sundown, so she sold everything, bought back the café, which had been closed for a year, and moved to town."

"I take it that you weren't happy with the decision," Dan commented upon hearing the bitterness in her voice.

"No. Though my brothers had lived in town before and really liked it, I'd never known anything but farm life. I hated our duplex, hated the café, hated the fact that things had to change. It isn't—" She caught herself, blushing. "I mean *wasn't* fair. My brothers should have pitched in and helped Mom. That farm was as much a part of their heritage as mine."

"What do they do now?" Dan asked. Intensely aware of her slip of the tongue and misty eyes, he believed he now understood her obsession with the house. And while he sympathized with Torie to a degree, his heart went out to her mother and brothers, as well.

"Mack teaches English at the University of Tennessee at Knoxville. He also writes children's books. Richard is an accountant."

"So neither of them is very outdoorsy?"

"Well, Mack likes to go camping at least once a summer," she replied with a shrug.

"I guess you could call that outdoorsy, all right, but hardly farmer material."

Torie tensed at his words and glared at him, silently demanding, "Who asked you?" Aloud she said nothing, however. Getting to her feet, she brushed off the jeans she wore over today's lavender leotard.

"I can see that you agree with my mother's decision," she said, those same eyes now nailing Dan to the floor. "Perhaps you're both right. I don't really know. I do know that when Mom sold the farm, my life changed for the worse. I promised myself then that I would someday own every acre of it again, find myself a mate who loved it as much as I did, and begin a dynasty of my own. And while it looks as though I might have to modify my plans somewhat, you can rest assured that I haven't given all of them up."

"Does that mean you still want to marry, play housewife and raise a passel of kids?"

"And what's wrong with that?"

"Nothing. I just didn't think there was a woman alive today with such old-fashioned dreams."

"Old-fashioned or not, they're mine," Torie snapped. "I should have known they'd sound tame to you."

Actually they sounded wonderful, and resurrected some old-fashioned dreams of Dan's own. He had no intentions of admitting that, though. What was the point? Torie obviously wanted to share her life with a husband exactly like the father she adored, and he wasn't applying for the job.

Actually regretting that he'd goaded her into this most recent altercation, Dan reached up to capture her hand and her attention. "You know, Torie Hanover," he said, "we've got a heck of a lot in common."

She laughed shortly and tugged her fingers free. "Besides the fact that we both want this house, I can't think of a single thing."

"Well, I can," Dan told her. "We've both lost our fathers, for one thing."

Torie gave him a long look and then sat back down. "How did your dad die?"

"A heart attack . . . two weeks before I turned eighteen. He and I had been waiting for that birthday for five years. I was going to move to Tennessee to live with him."

"You didn't like living with your mom?"

"I didn't like *not* living with my dad," Dan said, unwilling to enlarge on that.

"I'm sure he missed you just as much."

"You're damn right he did. He couldn't wait for me to get there. He had my room all ready. Hell, he'd already bought the plane ticket."

"Oh, Dan," Torie murmured, turning and engulfing him in an unexpected hug. "I'm really sorry."

He shrugged in reply, touched by her sympathy, then willingly returned the embrace. "It was a long time ago," he said into her hair.

"But we never forget."

"No," he said, his own eyes suddenly brimming. "We never forget."

They sat in companionable silence for a moment—Torie with her cheek resting on Dan's collarbone, Dan with his chin propped on her head. Relaxed, relishing the novel peace, Dan breathed deeply of the scent that was Torie—a potpourri of fresh air, flowers and irresistible woman.

The fragrance filled his head and lungs, beguiling him. Intrigued by his intense reaction to it and perhaps a little drunk on the heady incense, Dan touched his lips to Torie's temple. She sighed softly and melted against him, a move that flattened her full breasts against his chest and his thudding heart.

At once overwhelmed by her nearness, yet wanting to be closer still, Dan tightened the embrace. He tangled his fingers in Torie's curls, tugging gently to tip her head back. Her gaze locked with his.

Dan caught his breath at the glow of what just might be desire in those wide blue eyes. Torie's answering gasp told him that his own yearning must be every bit as evident.

"I'd really like to kiss you," he told her, ever mindful of her negative reaction to him the night before.

"What are you waiting for?"

Hungrily their mouths met and melded. Boldly he traced the fullness of Torie's lips with his tongue, alternately teasing and thrusting until she parted them and gave him full access to the sweet interior of her mouth. Dan deepened the kiss, savoring her flavor, which was every bit as fascinating as her fragrance. Taking Torie with him, he lay slowly back on the floor, where a calculated twist of his body put her partially beneath him and away from the danger of the open stairwell.

Dan positioned his forearms on either side of Torie to take his weight before trailing his lips across her cheek and down to the throbbing pulse in her neck. She moaned in response, then shivered, moving restlessly against him. Fearing she might be uncomfortable lying there on the dusty wooden floor, Dan raised his head so he could read her expression.

But he never got the chance. Murmuring her displeasure at the inches now between them, Torie pulled him back within reach, then kissed him with a fever that consumed rational thought and left him whirling helplessly in an eddy of sensation.

She was pure magic, and Dan willingly abandoned himself to her charms. Never had anyone so enchanted him. Never. Spellbound, lost in the wonder of it all, he wasn't a bit surprised when he suddenly heard bells ringing.

And why should he be?

A man was *supposed* to hear bells when he kissed the woman of his dreams.

Chapter Five

Woman of his dreams?

Dan jackknifed to his feet. Putting as much distance between himself and Torie as the tiny room would allow, he stood with his back to the wall, sucking air into lungs that had ceased to function.

"What is it?" Torie instantly demanded, her eyes huge with bewilderment. She sat up abruptly, tossing her moon-kissed curls back over her shoulder. Dan's gaze swept over the lavender leotard hugging her upper body, lingering on the taut tips of her breasts, which strained against the shimmering fabric.

That evidence of her arousal merely made his own worse, adding to his distress. Sex—that was all he wanted from this woman. Uncomplicated, mind-boggling sex. Instead, he'd heard bells. Still heard them, in fact.

Tensing at that realization, Dan listened more closely. Then, with a grunt of discovery, he turned and busied himself trying to open the hinged window.

"Dan!" Torie exclaimed with impatience. *"What is wrong?"*

"I hear bells," he answered, as if that explained everything.

"Of course you do," she said, throwing up her arms in exasperation. One minute, he was kissing her out of her mind, the next, he was climbing the wall. Now he had his head stuck out the window. She couldn't keep up with him! "I hear them, too. The church bell is chiming the hour, just like it always does. It's—" she glanced at her watch "—oh, my God!"

Scooting on her rear toward the stairwell, Torie put her feet on the steps and began to scramble down them as quickly as safety—and the cobwebs—would allow.

"Where are you going?" Dan called from above her. She heard his heavy footfall on the hardwood floor, felt the steps give when he followed.

"Rush," she tossed over her shoulder as she put a foot on solid ground and headed right on down the hall. "I've got a dance class starting in less than thirty minutes."

"You'll never make it."

"Wanna bet?" Torie muttered under her breath. After descending the stairs in a manner reminiscent of Mack, she dashed across the living room and yanked open the door. In a heartbeat she was outside and leaping off the porch, her car dead in her sights.

"For Pete's sake, Torie," Dan yelled from behind her. "Wait up."

"Can't," she replied, never breaking stride.

"But what about your lunch?" He was right beside her now, and one quick step put him directly in her path.

Torie stumbled to a halt. "There isn't time," she said, trying to step around him to open the car door.

Dan moved first to the right and then to the left to block her path. "You have to eat."

Torie huffed her exasperation with him. "I'll eat tonight."

"As much as you did at your mom's Monday night?" he demanded, glowering at her.

Surprised by his blatant concern, Torie halted her struggle to get to the car. "I wasn't hungry, then. I will be tonight. Now quit worrying. I ate breakfast this morning."

"Yeah? What'd you eat?"

"Cookies and milk," she mumbled rather hesitantly, half expecting a lecture on nutrition. Instead, she got one of those gypsy smiles that did amazing things to her blood pressure.

"Can't fault that, I guess," Dan said. "But you really should eat a good meal tonight. You're a growing girl."

"Lord, I hope not," she replied with a glance down the body she struggled to keep in shape.

Dan's gaze followed hers, lingering where it had no business, gentle as a caress. Torie's pulse, just returning to normal from her jog and those mind-bending kisses preceding it, went berserk again.

"Have dinner with me tonight."

Dinner? With *him?* Torie gulped, at once sure that wasn't a good idea.

"I owe you a meal, after all," he added, capturing her shoulders in his big hands, squeezing gently. To Torie's surprise, he dropped his head down so that his forehead touched hers.

"You don't owe me anything," she murmured, disconcertingly aware of his proximity. She recognized the scent of his cologne—Risk—and decided it aptly described the man.

"Well, you owe me," Dan retorted. "Last night you volunteered your services as hostess, guide and whatever else it would take to make me feel at home. Tonight it's going to take a dining companion. I don't want to eat alone."

Torie hesitated. True, she had volunteered, but that was before last night's kiss, and today's . . . what? What really would have happened if Dan hadn't heard bells? Would they now be lying on the floor of her father's old office, bodies deliciously bare, making slow, sweet love?

Love, my foot! she scolded, deliberately blocking out that intriguing scenario. What had happened between them moments ago had nothing whatsoever to do with love, and she knew it. It was time—yet again—to get her head on straight. Dan Stewart had a house she wanted. Her sole purpose for spending time with him was to get it back. Tonight would be a perfect opportunity to try to do that.

"Then, of course, I'll eat with you."

He smiled his delight. "Pick you up at six?"

"Six is fine." She ducked under his arm and reached for the door.

"You'd better brush off before you go," Dan said. "Your backside is covered with dust."

"Oh, dear," Torie murmured, swiping her hand over her shoulders. To her dismay, Dan helped out, stopping just above her derriere.

"Um, maybe you'd better get the rest," he mumbled, stepping back and tucking his fingers into the pockets of his jeans.

When Torie finished and passed inspection, Dan glanced at his watch. "Ten after twelve. It'll be a wire job, but you can probably make your class on time."

Torie, who could drive the road to Rush blindfolded and knew the state trooper's usual hideout, merely grinned and got into the car, shutting the door behind her. Dan bent down to peer in the window, his brown eyes narrowed in suspicion.

"Keep it legal, Torie. Speed kills."

"That? From you?" With a short laugh, she started the engine, put the car in gear and left him standing in a cloud of dust and black exhaust.

Speed kills. His words echoed loudly in her head as she whizzed along, bringing a blush to her cheeks. Speed did, indeed, kill. On the highway and on the dusty floor of an antiquated house.

Deliberately she replayed those forbidden moments in the attic. She remembered how it felt to have Dan so close, his considerable weight pinning her to the floor. What a warm, safe sensation.

Safe? Torie laughed aloud, marveling at the power of sex. If she actually thought it was "safe" to be lying, pliant as putty, under Dan Stewart, she was in worse shape than she'd thought.

What is wrong with me? she wondered, thoroughly shocked at her wanton actions. A virgin and proud of it, Torie had never understood why a woman would give herself to any man but the one with whom she intended to spend the rest of her life. Now that she'd met Dan, she knew.

Once she'd thought him temptation with a capital everything. Now she thought him male with a capital *M,* intriguing with a capital *I* and sexy with a capital *S*. If she added a *T-A-K-E*—which was what he'd do with her precious innocence if she let him—she'd have MISTAKE. A very big one.

She and Dan had different goals in life. He did not want to marry, to have children, to put down roots. There was no point in spending any more time with him than what was absolutely necessary to wrangle the house away. It made no sense to kiss, hold and lust after him.

So why did her lips still tingle, her heart race? Why did she have this knot in the pit of her stomach and the empty ache just below it?

And why was she racking her brain to figure out what to wear tonight?

Dan checked his look in the mirror one more time and then snorted his disgust with himself. He was acting like an inexperienced kid, for Pete's sake. Not the mature adult he really was.

Mature adult? Yeah, right.

Groaning, Dan plopped down on the couch and covered his eyes with his hands. For the umpteenth time he relived the afternoon's fiasco with Torie. For the umpteenth time, his body responded to the memory of her flavor and fragrance. What a woman. She drove him out of his ever-loving mind.

And judging from her passionate kisses yesterday, he did a few things to hers, as well. Why else had she lain on the floor and made out with a man whose life-style and goals she so clearly despised?

Dan didn't know. He did know that it wasn't right to take advantage of her confusion. She had made it plain that she wanted love, marriage and children—*in that order*. He did not have similar hopes and dreams. He had learned the hard way that those things were not for him.

His parents' split and his own disastrous marriage early in his driving career had left him sadder but wiser. Forever afters were obviously not for everyone. That realized, Dan had buried himself in his career and learned to find satisfaction in being constantly on the go, a life-style that suited him to a T . . . most of the time.

There were nights when he wished he didn't have wheels under his bed, nights when a shingle roof would have been nice overhead. There were even nights when he would have welcomed the conversation of a wife, the commotion of a couple of kids. But for all those nights, he was still not the kind of man who could settle down for any length of time and be content. He certainly wasn't the kind of man who could make Torie happy on a long-term basis. As for short term, well, that was something else altogether.

Dan honestly believed they could have a good time, but only if he laid his cards on the table. The "mature adult" in him would accept nothing less than total honesty. He was willing to give Torie his body, sans heart and for a limited time only. Nothing more. She had to understand what she was getting into.

But first things first. Before he dared appeal to the passion he'd glimpsed inside Torie, he would have to teach her to appreciate who and what he was—a racer who loved his mobility. There was no doubt in his mind that might prove more challenging than any race he'd ever driven. And for that reason he'd better have a plan in his pocket when he picked her up that night.

Though fully prepared to dine at her mother's café, just about the only choice in England, Torie donned her best—a creamy silk shirtwaist with an ornate gold belt. Wide loop earrings and a matching bracelet completed her outfit and added an air of elegance she hoped Dan would find impressive.

Why she wanted to impress him, Torie couldn't imagine. She told herself it had something to do with the fact that he'd never seen her in anything but a leotard. Unfortunately that didn't explain why she spent a solid hour washing, drying and curling her hair.

Dan arrived promptly at six, dressed in a wheat-colored cotton sweater, with flecks of golden brown the exact shade of his eyes. His pants, pleated at the waist, fit to perfection and drew her gaze downward the length of his long legs to his snakeskin boots.

It was difficult to drag her eyes away from such an awesome sight, but Torie did—at least long enough to get her clutch bag. Together, they walked to his truck. Torie eyed the massive vehicle with some trepidation, wishing she'd worn slacks instead of a skirt. But Dan didn't seem the least concerned, and acting as if it were the most natural thing in the world to do, opened the door on the passenger side, lifted her up in his arms and deposited her on the seat.

Moments later he was behind the wheel, backing out of the trailer park and heading down the highway—away from Erma's Eatery.

"Where are we going?" Torie instantly demanded.

"To Knoxville."

"But that's over a hundred miles away!" she exclaimed, thunderstruck.

Dan laughed. "I love to drive, always have. This truck my sponsors gave me is a dream to drive. We'll be there in no time."

"But where will we eat? I'm not at all familiar with Knoxville."

"Relax. That's my old stomping ground."

"I thought you were from Florida."

"Only these days. I'm Tennessee-born and -bred. Lived in Knoxville until I joined the navy at nineteen."

"I didn't know you were in the navy," Torie murmured, adding, "My uncle was, too. He was a Seabee. What did you do?"

"I worked on fighter jets."

"Is that where you got your love of engines and speed?"

"What is this?" Dan asked with a grin. "Trivial Pursuit?"

Torie laughed. "Uh-huh, and the category is Dan Stewart."

"In that case, I'll answer your question. I got my love of speed and engines from my dad. There wasn't a motor in existence that he couldn't tear down and put back together, and he taught me everything he knew. Would you believe I rebuilt my first engine when I was six?"

"Nope," Torie told him without hesitation.

"Hmm. How about nine? Would you believe nine?"

Torie gauged his sincerity and then shook her head. "Uh-uh."

"Well, then, would you buy twelve?" Dan asked.

"Now twelve, I'll buy," she told him with a brisk nod.

"I knew you had a head on those shoulders." His teasing smile was just visible in the dusky interior of the truck. "And while we're on the subject of buying, got any use for a bridge? I just happen to own a really big one. . . ."

So she'd been taken, after all. Drawing on the experience of a lifetime spent with mischievous males, Torie landed a playful punch on Dan's shoulder. Laughing, he caught her hand and tugged on it, propelling her right across the vinyl seat and almost into his lap. When she would have scooted back, he halted her with a brisk, "Stay."

Torie did . . . all too willingly.

Silence reigned for several miles, comfortable silence that Torie relished as much as their newfound, unexpected closeness. Dan turned on the radio, and then, to the muted background of a country rock song, talked about his five years in the navy and nine on the NASCAR circuit, first on a pit crew and then as a driver. Torie listened with growing sadness at the details of his nomadic life-style, a life-style he obviously loved.

How he could tolerate such an existence she simply didn't know. She cherished the security of her roots, which provided a firm foundation for her goals of marriage and family. Dan had similar roots, for all his mobility now. And though his parents' divorce had lent an element of instability to his childhood, he'd nevertheless spent more than half his life in one city.

So why were their outlooks so different?

What had happened to put Dan Stewart on the move? Was he running from something? Or to it?

Torie couldn't be sure, and wondered if his restlessness resulted not from a love of adventure but an old-as-mankind search for hearth and home. Though Dan might not ever admit it or even realize it, his goals might be the same as hers. At the thought, her traitorous heart swelled with something very much like joy.

But how would she ever get Dan to consider the possibility? And more important, why would she even want to?

"I love driving at night," Dan murmured at that moment. "Love the sight of that center line stretching to forever."

Torie heaved a mental sigh and banished to regions unknown any foolish notions of trying to tune Dan's brain to her wavelength. For whatever reason, he had a gypsy soul. They would never see eye to eye.

She'd do well to stick to the business at hand.

The restaurant, located lakeside in an obviously well-to-do section of town, proved delightful. After leading Dan and Torie around the edges of the dance floor and seating them at a secluded table for two, the hostess left the wine list and disappeared. Torie glanced all around, taking appreciative note of the snow white linen tablecloth, lighted tapers and sparkling crystal goblets before her. Lovely, she thought, and not in the least conducive to a levelheaded campaign to talk Dan Stewart out of his house.

The saxophone playing softly in the background did nothing to dispel the air of intimacy that had cloaked them the moment they stepped into the restaurant. It did, however, make Torie extremely nervous. There was nothing like that sexy moan to loosen a fanciful young woman's inhibitions. Sticking to the business at hand was going to be damned difficult.

"Do you want a glass of wine?" Dan asked, breaking into her thoughts. Torie realized with a start that a waitress had joined them and stood waiting to take their drink order.

"Do you?"

"I'm designated driver," he told her with a grin. "But you can certainly have some."

"I'd just as soon have a glass of iced tea," she said, not adding that she was stimulated enough already.

Dan ordered a cup of coffee for himself. After the waitress left, he leaned toward Torie, eyes twinkling. "So what do you think? Do I know my Knoxville restaurants or not?"

"You know them," she said. "Everything is perfect."

He grinned his pleasure. "Glad you like it. I come here every time I'm in town."

"Are you in town often?" Torie asked.

"Every two or three months I whip through. My mom still lives here with my stepdad."

"And you're on good terms with her?"

Dan shrugged. "I don't blame her for the divorce, if that's what you're asking. As for being on good terms, I guess you could say we are. We're certainly not on bad

terms. She had her own life to live, I have mine. We're not particularly close these days, but then we never were—at least not as close as my dad and I."

This revelation didn't come as a surprise and merely increased Torie's growing belief that Dan was running to, not from, love. Impulsively she reached out and covered his hand with hers. She squeezed it gently, an action that drew his gaze. They exchanged a long, heart-stopping look, before he eased his hand free and picked up the menu the waitress had left them.

"Hungry?"

"Starved," she admitted, reaching for her own menu. Quickly she scanned it, noting that all of the offerings were in French and none of them had prices listed. "How are we supposed to know how much anything costs?" she whispered, leaning across the tiny table toward Dan.

He lowered his menu and closed the distance between them until their noses were almost touching. "*We* aren't. *I* am." Grinning, Dan showed her his menu, which had the prices—exorbitant prices—clearly noted.

"Let's swap," Torie suggested, horrified to find that a simple chicken dish cost over thirty dollars. She had no intention of ordering, much less eating, anything so outrageously expensive.

Dan laughed at that and shook his head. "No way, honey. I want you to order whatever you want tonight without guilt. I owe you, remember? And besides, we're celebrating."

"What are we celebrating?"

"Our friendship."

Friendship, my foot, she thought, eyeing him and then their romantic surroundings with growing alarm. A fool could see Dan had more than friendship on his mind, and

Torie Hanover was evidently one of the biggest fools around.

Why else would she be over a hundred miles from home with a man she found so irresistible? Because he owed her a meal? Fat chance. The time she'd donated today was worth little more than a greasy-spoon hamburger and a side of fries. If Torie wined and dined as elegantly as Dan intended her to, she would end up owing *him*.

There was no doubt in her mind what Dan might want in payment. And there was no doubt in her mind that he'd get what he wanted.

"So what's your pleasure?"

Torie jumped at the sound of Dan's voice, then gave him a nervous smile. "I'm really not very hungry."

"But you just told me you were starved," he said. He sat in silence for a moment, frowning. "Are you having trouble reading the menu? Because if that's it, we can get the waitress to interpret. I always order the same thing when I come here, so it's never a problem with me."

"I had two years of French in college," Torie said. "I can read the menu."

"You went to college?" Dan asked, clearly startled.

Torie bristled at his tone. "The University of Arkansas at Little Rock. I have a degree in the performing arts."

"You're just full of surprises," he murmured, leaning back in his chair and crossing his arms over his chest.

"What's that supposed to mean?" Torie demanded.

"It means I never dreamed you could tear yourself away from England long enough to get a degree."

So he thought she'd spent her entire life on a three-mile stretch of Tennessee highway. "For your information, I lived in New York six weeks last summer, studying ballet. I've been as far west as San Francisco, as far south as Tijuana, and as far north as Alberta, Canada."

"Any place else?" Dan interjected, with what could only be a smile teasing the corners of his mouth.

"Charlotte, North Carolina. I went to a Winston Cup race with my brothers and an uncle when I was little."

"Want to go again? I'm leaving on Saturday."

"Stop teasing me!" she exclaimed.

"I'm not," he told her.

"Yes, you are," Torie said. She threw down her menu and propped her elbows on the table. Hiding her face in her hands, she murmured, "I should never have come here with you tonight."

"Why did you?" Dan asked softly.

"Because I want your house," Torie snapped. Dead silence followed that thoughtless admission. Horrified at what she'd said, Torie peeked through her fingers at Dan, who watched her intently.

She gulped and raised her gaze to meet his. "I can't believe I said that."

"It's true?"

She hesitated. "Sort of."

"What do you mean 'sort of'?"

"Well...I probably would've come with you tonight even if I hadn't had an ulterior motive."

"Because you're really hungry, after all?"

"Because I find you a fascinating man, Dan Stewart. I've never met anyone quite like you."

Dan sat without speaking for a moment, head tilted slightly to one side as he studied her thoughtfully. "You've got five minutes."

"Excuse me?"

"Five minutes and not a second more. You'd better start talking."

"About what?" she asked, thoroughly baffled.

"My house," he replied. "Your town. Whatever else you think will convince me to sell. Then I don't want to hear another word about it tonight."

Torie's jaw dropped. Stunned speechless, she could do no more than gape at her dinner companion.

"Time's a wastin'," he prompted, eyes on his watch.

She came to life immediately, words tumbling off her tongue in her haste to get everything said. "We have terrible winters in England. If you move into that house you'll have to deal with a winding highway and icy graveled side roads."

"My truck is a four-by-four," Dan replied. "And I'm a damn good driver. Transportation won't be a problem."

Before she could reply, the waitress arrived to take their orders. Since Torie hadn't even given the menu a second glance and now had something more important on her mind, she let Dan select for her. The moment they were alone again, she glanced at her watch. "That minute won't count against me, will it?"

Dan shook his head quite solemnly, but his eyes twinkled.

"Good." Unwilling to be sidetracked by anger, Torie deliberately ignored that hint of amusement and plunged ahead. "Your neighbor to the east has cows that get out of the pasture all the time. Why, it's nothing to wake up and find that your flower bed has been nibbled to the ground."

"That's okay. I'm not really into flower beds."

"But the cows leave holes in the ground where they graze. You could break an ankle or maybe even a leg in one. You wouldn't be able to drive."

"I promise I'll watch my step."

"You'd better. Tracks are not the only calling card you're going to find in your yard."

"So what's a little fertilizer left lying here and there? It'll just make the grass grow."

"Grass that will be heck to mow with all those holes in the yard."

"I assure you, I'll manage."

He sounded as though he meant it, and momentarily daunted, Torie hesitated before plunging ahead. "Your neighbor to the west has chickens—lots of chickens. And geese. You'll find them roosting under the porch, in the well house, on your truck."

"How convenient," Dan replied. "I do love fresh eggs."

"But he has goats, too. Goats that eat any and everything."

"Even grass?"

"Especially grass."

"Good. That takes care of the mowing problem."

Torie could have strangled him. "Damn it, Dan, you're making jokes and I'm serious. England is not Daytona Beach."

"Exactly the reason I want to live there. Now your time is up, Ms. Hanover. Let's dance."

"Dance?" She couldn't believe her ears.

"Dance." Dan got to his feet and pulled her to hers. Dazed, Torie let him lead her onto the nearby dance floor. "Hold me," he said as he did exactly that to her.

Torie hesitated, then put one hand on his waist and laid the other lightly on his shoulder. Dan began to sway to the music, moving his feet in a manner reminiscent of what Torie had always called the high-school shuffle.

"I guess you can tell I don't dance," he said, just as he stepped on her toe.

"You could've—ouch—fooled me," she lied.

"Sorry."

"No—oops—problem."

"Maybe we'd better sit this one out."

"You're doing fine. Just relax and let the music take you."

"Take me where?" he asked.

"Wherever you want to go."

"Will you come with me?"

"Do you want me to?"

"I want you to."

"Then I'll come."

Dan sighed as if their foolishness had actually settled something. Visibly relaxing, he pulled her closer. Torie rested her cheek on his shoulder, relishing the sensation of being heart-to-heart with him once again.

"This is nice," he murmured against her hair an eternity later.

"Mmm-hmm," she agreed, eyes closed.

"No wonder your brother and his family take you camping with them. You make a great traveling companion."

Torie smiled into his sweater. "Actually, you're not half bad yourself."

"Yeah?"

"Yeah."

"Does that mean you'll go to Charlotte with me?"

"You were serious?" Torie blurted, raising her head to peruse Dan's face. He looked as though he meant what he said, and unsure of his motives for such an astounding invitation—not to mention the ramifications of it—she sidestepped the issue. "Is that the last race of the season?"

"No. There's one more after this one."

"And then you settle in England for the winter?"

"No, then I make another truck commercial."

"How'd you get started in those?" Torie asked.

"The company that makes my truck also sponsors my race car. The commercials are part of our deal."

"I see. And after you finish the commercial?"

"*Then* I settle in my house for the winter."

It was Torie's turn to sigh. "Correct me if I'm wrong. You race thirty-nine Sundays out of the year, beginning in February."

"Every once in a while they're on Saturday," her companion interjected.

She ignored him. "At the first of the season, the races are a week apart. At the end—I believe the last three races—they're two weeks apart."

Dan's eyes rounded in surprise, but he didn't speak.

"And since the races are all over the South," Torie steadfastly continued, "you spend the early part of the week after each one getting to the next state, and the latter part of the week on practice and time trials once you get there."

"How do you know all that?" Dan interjected. "Are you a racing fan?"

"Never mind. My point is that you never would've spotted the house on Monday if you hadn't been en route from one race to the next. And while you've actually managed to spend a whole week in England, that much free time isn't normal for the majority of the racing season. You're wasting your money restoring that house, Dan Stewart. You won't be home long enough to enjoy it."

"I don't intend to race forever," Dan said, clearly bristling.

Torie's heart skipped a beat. "You don't?"

"Of course not. Someday, when I'm old and gray, I'll retire and live there all year round."

A lot of good that will do me, Torie silently grumbled, immediately berating herself for that off-the-wall thought.

Aloud she said, "Oh, yeah. You did tell me you intended to find yourself a good dog and live to a ripe old age in that house." She shook her head. "A good woman would be a lot more fun, you know. And if you'd like to reconsider on your proposed housemate, I'll invite every eligible female in England—if I can find any—to your party Friday night."

"There's at least one," Dan reminded her, halting the dance as the last strains of music died. He took her hand off his shoulder and raising it to mouth level, kissed her palm and the tip of each finger.

Torie's bones turned to jelly. "I'm not in the running," she gasped, clutching the back of his sweater to stay upright. In truth, she was ready to put her name at the top of the list of eligible women Dan had no intentions of marrying. He was so damned charming, and she saw so many good qualities in him—if not exactly the qualities she sought.

"I see," he murmured. The music began again, and once more moving to the drugging beat, Dan added, "Don't waste your time trying to find me a mate. I have no intentions of getting married again."

"Again?" Torie squeaked. This time it was she who did the toe treading.

"Ouch."

"Sorry. I, uh, didn't know you were divorced."

"That's not surprising. I don't like to talk about it."

"How long were you married?"

"One racing season."

"What happened?"

"I'm not sure. I guess she got tired of sleeping single in a double bed."

"Did you love her?"

"Apparently not. I couldn't give up the racing when she asked me to."

"I'm sorry."

"For me or for her?"

"For you."

"Don't be. The whole thing was my fault. No one forced me to stay on the road all the time. I deserved what happened. And since my situation hasn't changed, you must understand why another wife is out of the question."

"You can't let one little mistake govern your whole future," Torie argued. "Maybe you chose the wrong woman."

"And what kind of woman should a rolling stone like me have selected?"

"One willing to accept you for what you are, of course," she blurted, much to her own astonishment. "One willing to keep the home fires burning."

"Or one willing to give up everything and go on the road with me?"

She shrugged and avoided his questioning gaze. "I—I suppose so."

"Know any angels like that?" Dan asked with a short laugh.

Torie searched her heart and came up lacking. "No," she murmured softly, shaking her head.

"I thought not. Does that mean that Charlotte is out of the question?"

"Yes." Her voice was now just a whisper.

"I thought as much." Dan stopped dancing and glanced toward the table. "There's our food. We'd better eat and hit the road. Something tells me it's going to be a long drive home."

98 19/19 19 pages

Chapter Six

In actuality, it wasn't.

By the time Dan and Torie left the restaurant and got into his truck, they were laughing and joking exactly as they had on the trip up. Each made sure the lighter mood prevailed all the way back home by deliberately avoiding controversial issues such as old houses, marriages gone sour and impending races in Charlotte.

It was after midnight when the not-so-bright street-lights of England finally loomed in the dark up ahead. Silent for the first time in hours, Torie viewed those beacons with mixed emotions. She realized with surprise that she actually dreaded the moment when Dan would walk her to the door and leave with a handshake instead of a kiss.

That he would do exactly that, Torie had no doubts. She'd turned down his shocker of an invitation to Charlotte, after all. He now understood that she had no intentions of carrying their crazy relationship one smidgen past the comfortable amity they shared at this moment.

At least, she *hoped* he understood.

If, by some miracle, he hadn't gotten the picture yet and actually made an attempt to warm things up when they said good-night, Torie Hanover, with her mixed emotions and forbidden desires, was in big trouble. These past hours with Dan had been a joy, an oasis in the desert of her non-existent social life. And while a forever after with him was out of the question, a right-now tempted her something fierce.

Why, she couldn't understand. Torie considered herself an intelligent young woman who'd known for years exactly what she wanted from life and the kind of man who could give it to her. By his own admission, Dan Stewart was not that man. Therefore, a romance with him, however diverting, would be a shameful waste of time. At twenty-two, Torie believed she didn't have much of that to spare, not if she was going to fall in love, marry *and* have the four children she'd always wanted.

So why did Dan's invitation to Charlotte haunt her? Why did she wonder if she'd done the right thing in turning him down? Was it because she believed he'd issued it as a friend to a friend? Or because—intelligence and goals aside—she secretly hoped that friendship was the last thing on his mind?

Torie acknowledged that she simply didn't know, and for that reason welcomed the sight of their turnoff and an end to the evening. But to her astonishment, Dan didn't slow the truck. Instead, he accelerated and sped right on through England.

"That was our road," Torie exclaimed, twisting to watch it disappear into the night behind them.

"I know," Dan replied.

"Then why didn't you take it?"

"Because we're not ready to go home."

Torie tensed. "We're not?"

"No. Tonight has been really special. We're going to make it last just a little longer."

A mile later, Dan turned onto a narrow dirt trail that Torie knew led to an abandoned rock-quarry-turned-lake. Dubbed the "passion pit" by several decades of England parents, it was often the site of daytime picnics and late-night trysts. Torie, who'd parked here many times as a teenager and always stayed in control of the situation, thought the dangers of such romantic solitude highly exaggerated. She now eyed the moonlit area with pleasure. A cool breeze rippled the silver-plated water and sighed through the tall pines lining the shore. Tree frogs serenaded in a hypnotizing harmony.

There were no other cars at the lake. Whether because of the late hour or the day of the week, Torie didn't know or care. For the first time that night, she was totally alone with the most intriguing male she'd ever met, *and* she had his full attention. What woman in her right mind would let an opportunity like that slip away unacknowledged?

One kiss? she mused, as Dan killed the lights and the engine. One kiss, she decided, hopelessly lost to the magic of the lake, the moon and the man. One kiss, she sternly reminded herself as he slid across the seat into her waiting arms.

A truckload of kisses later, Torie knew why her mother had always warned her to stay clear of the pit. She also knew that her mother was wrong about the source of the danger. It wasn't a *where;* it was a *who*—a good-looking, sweet-talking, totally irresistible who.

The same *who* now nibbled her neck and collarbone.

Collarbone? Yes, indeed, and Torie's entire body tingled with anticipation of where his next kiss might fall.

Struggling to take charge of her humming hormones and his wandering hands, Torie gulped in a deep, calming breath. She framed Dan's face with her sweaty palms, deliberately guiding his gaze back above the neck.

"It's very late. We've got to go," she murmured, clutching together the neck of her dress and re-securing the top two buttons.

"We will," Dan murmured against her mouth even as he lifted her onto his lap.

"When?" Torie gasped, tilting her head to give him access to the sensitive flesh just below her ear. Dan grunted his satisfaction and rewarded her efforts with a series of shivery kisses that trailed from earlobe to bare shoulder.

Bare shoulder? Damn those wanton buttons. "When, Dan?"

"Soon."

"How soon?"

Dan raised his head, looked her dead in the eye and smiled. "As soon as you say the word."

Torie bristled at his smug expression, wondering if he thought her so far gone that she couldn't call a halt to his seduction. She opened her mouth to reply but words were forgotten when the heat of Dan's hand penetrated the silk skirt draped over her thigh.

Instead of giving Dan a big, fat "Now," she moaned softly. And clearly taking that reply as a "Not just yet," he kissed her again.

Another truckload of kisses later, Torie admitted she just might have lost control of the situation. Though still fully clothed, she lay flat on her back on the seat of the truck, Dan full on top of her—an amazing feat even in his spacious vehicle. Pulse rate out of control, hormones in hyperdrive, Torie gloried in the forbidden sensations shimmying up and down her spine. Dan's "Ah's" and

"Mmm's" told her he was most likely having a darn good time, too.

You've got to stop, Victoria Leigh Hanover, she told herself. *You've got to say, "Now."*

"I want you, Torie."

Dan wanted her? Well, she wanted him, too... as she'd wanted no other man. Suddenly the word *now* took on another meaning, and Torie knew if she uttered it, they would not be leaving the lake anytime soon. Throwing caution to the pines, she opened her mouth to echo his desire.

"And I—"

The whine of an approaching vehicle drowned her words. With a groan, Dan sat bolt upright. Cursing, he glared at the car bouncing and winding its way up the rugged path. Frantically he tugged Torie over and scrambled behind the wheel.

The powerful engine roared to life a heartbeat later. Torie winced at the sound, which sobered her as thoroughly as a splash of cold water.

Ducking out of sight behind the dash as they passed the approaching car—she knew every man, woman and teenager in England, after all—Torie thanked her lucky stars for the timely intrusion, which had undoubtedly saved her.

Dan was not so thankful. After muttering every expletive Torie had ever heard—and a few she hadn't—he sucked in several deep breaths, swallowed audibly and asked, "Your place or mine?"

"Neither," Torie told him as she sat back up and glared out the rear window at the barely visible sedan now parked by the lake a good distance behind them. She didn't recognize it, thank goodness. Maybe no harm had been done. She turned her full attention back to Dan, who guided the vehicle between two trees and stomped the brake pedal.

"What are you saying to me?" he demanded, clearly stunned.

"I'm saying that was a mistake," she told him.

With a flick of the wrist, Dan silenced the engine. He then switched off all lights but those on the dash, and laying an arm along the back of the seat, twisted to face her. "Want to tell me why?"

The surrounding woods, dark and suddenly ominous, pressed in on the truck. At once smothered, Torie rolled down her window a few inches and inhaled an autumn-scented breath. Then, feeling a little better, she turned back to Dan. "England is a little town. Everyone knows everyone else's business."

"So?"

"So if we get involved—and probably if we don't—we'll be the subject of every coffee break for the next ten years. That's the way little towns are."

"Who cares?"

"I do," Torie snapped. "I have to live here all year round, you know. Not just a few months of the year. My reputation is probably in shreds already, depending upon who was in that car that just surprised us. You'll be darned lucky if you don't wake up tomorrow morning with a shotgun tickling your ribs."

"One of your brothers?" Dan asked.

"Or my mother," Torie told him.

"But your mother likes me," he protested.

"In her café, maybe. Not in my bed."

Startled to silence by what was almost certainly truth, Dan considered shotgun weddings. To his surprise, one of those didn't sound so very terrible, and not just because of his highly aroused state. Dan searched his heart and found, deep inside it, a sense of belonging that had been foreign to him for a very long time.

It was almost as though he'd found more than a house in England. It was almost as though he'd found a home.

Dan frowned, suddenly distressed and uncomfortable. It had taken years to find happiness with his nomadic lifestyle, and three short days to lose it. Was he really willing to invite Torie into his life, thereby risking that tormenting metamorphosis again?

Deliberately turning his thoughts back in time, Dan called to mind the day his parents' divorce became final. His mother had remarried the next afternoon and taken him to live with a stepfather and his two young sons, who quickly stole the time and affection that should have been his. How jealous he'd been, how resentful. As though it were yesterday, he relived his misery and his subsequent determination to move in with his dad, who still loved him.

Dan also remembered the telephone call telling him his precious dad had died, and, along with him, their big plans to share an apartment and "batch it." That untimely death had haunted him, very nearly destroying his ability to love again, but he *had* loved again and then received a "Dear John" letter for his efforts. As always, these memories cut Dan like a knife. He closed his eyes and tipped his head back against the window, focusing on the pain so that he would not forget and act the fool again.

"Dan?"

Torie's soft voice intruded into his reverie, redirecting but not quite breaking into it. Another memory surfaced. Dan saw himself as a kid, sitting beside his dad in that rocking, speeding train. He remembered the beauty of the Tennessee countryside, felt once again the tingle of anticipation as the engine rounded the bend. Dan saw the house—his house—and the girl, blond, laughing, waving. His heart constricted with something he could not name, something like longing or maybe . . . love.

Love.

The word echoed loudly in Dan's head and brought a sardonic smile to his lips. Love, hell. Torie might have been his childhood fantasy, but she was not his adult reality. What had drawn them together tonight was purely physical, at least for him. He wasn't at all sure what her motives were.

"Dan? Are you all right?"

"I'm fine," he said, coming abruptly to life as one possible motive hit him in the gut. There had been several times in the past hour when Dan wondered if Torie was as experienced as her fiery kisses seemed to indicate. Caught up in the magic of the moment, however, he'd ignored his doubts and easily convinced himself that these days there was no such thing as a twenty-two-year-old virgin. Now he wasn't so sure, and that told him much.

"Are you angry?" Torie asked.

"No."

"I really didn't mean to tease and not follow through. I just wasn't thinking of the consequences."

"Because you've never been in this situation before?" he asked sharply, pinning her to the seat with his eyes.

"Oh, no," Torie said, with a quick shake of her head. She avoided his searching gaze and looked out the window as though she could actually see something in the black surrounding them. "That's not why."

I'll bet, Dan thought, now sure he had her motives figured out. By her own admission, she'd dined with him tonight because she wanted his house. Was that also the reason she'd been so cooperative during their romantic interlude moments ago? Undoubtedly, he decided. She'd already made it clear what kind of man she wanted, after all, and even saved herself for him. Since they both knew Dan was not the man, there could be no motive for her near submission except an ulterior one. She was trying to charm him out of his house.

Dan studied Torie's profile for a long moment, then reached to start the engine, wondering just how far she would have gone if they hadn't been interrupted. Probably not much further, he decided, the reason she now refused to pick up where they left off. It seemed that her innocence, if not her integrity, had outweighed her desire for the house.

"Actually I wasn't thinking of the consequences, either," he murmured. "Good thing we stopped before things got out of hand."

"Yeah," she breathed with obvious relief, turning back to him with a half smile and an apologetic shrug.

Dan put the truck in motion. Deliberately keeping the conversation light during the jolting ride back to the highway and then all the way to the trailer park, he coaxed a full-fledged smile and then a laugh from Torie. By the time they stopped in front of her mobile home, a peace, of sorts, had been restored.

In silence, they stepped from the vehicle and walked to her door.

"Good night, Torie," Dan said when they reached it.

"Good night, and thanks for dinner. I had a really, um . . . nice time."

Her shy smile, her wide eyes, the tremor in her voice—all demonstrated clearly that she wouldn't turn down a kiss now that the two of them were safe on her front step. Oddly hurt by her duplicity, Dan found he didn't want another one of those half as bad as he wanted to go home and think.

"I had a *nice* time, too." He turned to leave.

"See you tomorrow?"

So she hadn't given up yet. "I'll be busy tomorrow...working on the house. I've got to round up a roofer, a carpenter, a plumber and a painter from somewhere."

"Oh," Torie shrugged. "I'll be busy, too, now that I think about it. I've got classes all day and your party to plan."

"Party?"

"Friday night. Had you forgotten?"

He had, indeed, but would never admit it. "No, of course not."

"Is eight-thirty all right with you? I thought we'd have it at Mom's, and she doesn't close until eight."

"That's fine."

"Then I'll see you on Friday."

"Friday," he murmured as he headed to his lonely house on wheels.

Barely an hour later, Torie swiped her moisture-coated mirror with a fluffy yellow towel and leaned across the sink to peruse her face for any traces of makeup she might have missed in the bath. Satisfied with what she saw, she swayed back on her heels and cocked her head to one side.

"So what's the worst that could happen if I made love with Dan Stewart?" she asked her steamy reflection. She really knew the answer. No matter how careful they were, everyone in England would find out what was going on. They always did. Even if the two of them met miles away, someone would undoubtedly spot his truck or her car. Someone else would see an exchanged smile or overhear a conversation, and someone else would put two and two together and come up with the truth.

Torie knew she could not live or love haunted by the fear of discovery.

Love? *Love?*

Stunned by the direction her thought had taken, Torie dropped down to sit on the edge of the tub. Where did that come from, she wondered. Had she actually fallen in love? And with Dan Stewart . . . the enemy?

Oh, no, she immediately decided, with a quick shake of her head. She was not in love. And the only reason such an idea had even occurred to her was because she needed an excuse for her shocking lack of morals from the moment she'd met the man. Well, there was no excuse, and it was past time to get a grip on her lust.

Dan Stewart had been nothing but trouble since he'd hit England. And immediately following Friday night's party—her last-ditch effort to cajole him out of his house—she intended to lock him out of her life forever.

That decided, Torie pulled on her nightshirt and padded barefoot to her bed, snatching up paper and pencil as she passed the phone. Sitting cross-legged on a blue-and-pink comforter, handmade by her Grandmother Hanover, Torie listed the people she wanted to invite to Dan's party.

A few moments later, she perused the names she'd come up with thus far—all couples well acquainted with the woes of country living. Torie had known each and every one of them for years and felt certain they would all come to the party, even on such short notice. To be sure, however, she decided to open her dance studio to their children and hire a reliable teenager to play baby-sitter.

Frowning at the list, Torie next mulled over whether or not she should add the names of some single females, as she had told Dan she would. She quickly decided against it, telling herself that he'd told her not to bother, after all.

Torie then made a list of groceries she would need. Since tomorrow's—or was it today's?—dance lesson was in Faulkner, a town with a really nice supermarket, she decided to do her party shopping there. All she needed were a few soft drinks, dips, chips and a deli tray, since her mother had promised to bake a pie and a cake for the occasion.

It was nearly three in the morning before Torie turned out her light and crawled between the sheets. It was just after seven when she woke to her alarm and the smell of coffee in the automatic pot. With a groan, she levered herself from the bed and dragged her weary body to the window. A quick peek through the ruffled blue curtains revealed that Dan's truck was not parked in front of his trailer.

So he really does have a busy day planned, Torie mused, smiling slightly in satisfaction. The next instant her smile vanished. What did she care that Dan Stewart wasn't angry about last night and therefore not avoiding her? He could do as he pleased, after all.

She wasn't interested in him—as an enemy, as a friend or most especially as a lover. All she wanted was his house, and surely after tonight she would know whether or not she was ever going to get it.

Dan pulled into the parking lot of Erma's Eatery and shut off the engine of his truck. He glanced at the luminous dial of his watch, noting it was only eight-fifteen. He had a few minutes to spare before he went inside the café—a few more minutes to think about what had happened between him and Torie Wednesday night.

Not that more time was going to help. It probably wouldn't. Never in his life had Dan experienced such mixed emotions regarding a female. On one hand, he was disturbed that she was not the all-American young woman of his lifelong fantasy. On the other, he was more than ready to take advantage of her lack of scruples.

And why not? He'd told her more than once that he did not intend to sell the house. He'd meant every word. If Torie still wanted to gamble that he'd change his mind, then who was he to argue? He could take her wager with a clear conscience. Never mind that there was a much simpler, infinitely more satisfying solution to their little problem, namely sharing the house. If Torie wouldn't spend the night in his trailer, then she certainly wouldn't do anything as drastic as that.

At least he didn't think she would.

Lost in a bold new idea, Dan stared at the lighted café without really seeing it. Could he possibly convince Torie that they could both get what they wanted if she simply moved into the house with him? he suddenly wondered. Torie would "have" the house; Dan would "have" Torie.

It was the perfect arrangement, and now that he thought about it, maybe not so inconceivable. From all indications, Torie chafed under a yoke of small-town morals. Why else would she be willing to make love in a pickup truck, but not in his bed? She wasn't afraid of offering her body for the house and maybe having a good time in the bargain. She was afraid of getting caught doing it.

That had to be the reason for her hot-and-then-cold attitude toward him. Nothing else made sense. And now that he finally understood Torie's dilemma, he knew how to help her out of it. All he had to do was persuade her to ignore the certain censure of her family and friends and put up with the likes of him a few months of every year.

Piece of cake.

Laughing like the crazy man he surely was, Dan pulled the key from the ignition, dropped it into the pocket of his leather aviator jacket and stepped out of the truck.

Ten-thirty found Torie working behind her mother's counter, which was laden with every tempting morsel

Faulkner's supermarket could provide. She eyed the food, then made a quick head count that told her there was twenty-two people present, among them Patty and her husband, Jerry. As Torie had predicted, every couple she'd asked had accepted her invitation and now stood or sat all around the room, which had been rearranged to accommodate a party.

Their laughter and chatter mingled with the lively music filtering through the walls from the dance studio where Erma, who wouldn't hear of hiring a baby-sitter, now held a pint-sized party of her own.

Surreptitiously Torie scanned her guests, pausing when she spotted Dan over in a corner. He looked marvelous tonight, every bit as dashing as he had the first time she laid eyes on him. She was no less impressed now that she knew how wonderful it felt to have his whisker-roughened cheek against her skin, his sensuous lips pressed to hers.

And she wasn't the only person affected by his rugged charm and winning smile. From the moment he'd made his appearance promptly at eight-thirty, he'd been the center of attention. Every man in the room had congratulated him on his last win, every woman on his commercials. The fact that he credited his success in racing to his pit crew and his truck campaign to a clever ad man only endeared him to his new friends.

Torie's efforts to guide the conversation to the perils of country living had proved futile. Using skill she had seen before, Dan had repeatedly turned the tide of conversation until everyone in the room sang the praises of England. As a result, she could gladly have strangled him, and even now took mental measure of his handsome neck.

At that moment, Dan grinned and winked. Torie realized with a start that he was looking her way, which meant those teasing actions were meant for her. Embarrassed, she shifted her gaze and pretended to be busy behind the counter.

"Caught you, didn't he?"

Torie whirled on Patty, who'd appeared from nowhere and now stood beside her, eyes twinkling. "I'm sure I don't know what you mean."

Patty laughed. "Never kid a kidder, honey. I've spent the past two hours watching Dan watch you. Now I want to know what's going on."

"Nothing," Torie exclaimed, busying herself refilling an already brimming basket of chips.

Patty rolled her eyes in response, took the bag from Torie and set it aside. "There's plenty of food out. Come talk to my better half. He's really down tonight."

"Yeah?" Torie followed her old friend to a table where Jerry sat sipping a cold drink. He smiled a greeting and patted the empty chairs on either side of him. Torie and Patty both sat.

"You look a little better than you did the last time I saw you," Jerry said, studying Torie's face.

"I am better," she told him with a shrug. To be sure he believed her, she added a smile to the white lie. "And what about you?"

"Oh, not bad for a has-been roofer."

"Has-been?"

"Yeah. I got fired today."

Torie caught her breath and glanced sharply at Patty. "Why?"

"Because I refused to take a job over in Murry. The hundred-mile drive twice a day would've killed us financially and I'm not leaving Patty alone at night."

"Oh, Jerry, I'm sorry," Torie murmured. "What are you going to do?"

"Patty's dad will need some help in his wrecking yard next month. She thinks she can support us until then."

"You're a roofer?"

Torie jumped at the sound of Dan's voice just behind her.

"That's right," Jerry said, glancing up at him.

"It just so happens I'm looking for a good one," Dan said, moving to join them at the table. "When could you start?"

Jerry laughed shortly. "Tomorrow?"

"Tomorrow is Saturday. How about Monday?"

"You mean you're serious?" Jerry, Patty and Torie all gaped at Dan, who nodded.

"I just spent half my day trying to convince some old codger that I can't wait six months to get my house reroofed," he told the three of them. "You bet I'm serious."

"Then you've got yourself a roofer," Jerry exclaimed with a laugh of disbelief, extending his hand across the table to his new boss.

"I hate to discuss details here," Dan said. "But we really need to, since I'm going out of town tomorrow for a week."

"No sweat. I'll hang around after the party," Jerry suggested. "We can talk then."

Dan nodded. "Thanks."

"Is that all you lacked having everything lined up?" Torie interjected. Though pleased Jerry was employed again and so quickly, she hated the thought of his actually going to work on the house. The more money Dan put into it, the less likely he was going to let it go.

With a look of disgust, Dan shook his head. "No. I found a plumber who can get to me at the end of the week, but the painter and carpenter won't be available until mid-May."

"What do you need a carpenter for?"

Dan turned to peer at his questioner, a tall blonde who held a sandwich in one hand and a cola in the other. Torie realized with some surprise that their table was now surrounded by most of her guests.

"I've got some repair work to do on my house, both inside and out," Dan told him. "The shutters, a few of the doors, the floors, ceilings, walls . . ."

The blonde nodded. "How do you feel about hiring a carpenter with a bad back?"

"He's able to work?"

"Yeah."

"Is he any good?"

"Damn good. He got hurt on the job a few months ago through no fault of his own and had to sue to get his bills paid. Now none of the local construction companies will hire him."

"What's his name?" Dan asked.

"Red Henderson. He's my brother-in-law."

"Think he'd be available tonight to talk with me about it?" Dan then asked.

The blonde grinned and exchanged a glance with the slender redheaded woman at his side. "What do you think, Lorie?"

She nodded eagerly. "He'll be available."

Clearly pleased, Dan scanned the faces around him, then flashed a hopeful smile. "I don't suppose anyone knows an unemployed painter?"

"No," Louis Meyers, a cousin of Torie's, answered, muscling his way through the crowd to Dan's table. "But I know an employed one who'd be willing to work evenings and weekends so his son could make a down payment on the motorbike he's been wanting."

"You?" Dan questioned.

"Me. Are you wanting the exterior or interior of the house painted?"

"Just the exterior right now," Dan said. "Do you think you could get to it this week?"

"No problem," Louis said. "I've got an electric sprayer, so it shouldn't take more than a week's worth of evenings to get you fixed up. Ralph White has one, too. If I can get him to help out, we'll get it done even faster than that."

"Call him," Dan said, with a brisk nod. He got to his feet and smiled all around, visibly excited. "This is great. Just great. I don't know how to thank you folks for being so friendly and helping me out. I thought England was special the first time I set foot in it. Now I know it is."

"We're glad to have you here," Jerry told him, a sentiment with which everyone enthusiastically agreed—everyone except Torie. Realizing there wasn't a soul in that room who would have anything less than wonderful to say about England now, she heaved a mental sigh and admitted defeat, once and for all. Dan had won—hands down, fair and square, by a mile. It was over. Finally over.

And to her surprise, she felt more relief than anything else.

"Think you're going to like rural life?" Patty's question burst into Torie's abstraction.

"I can only think of one reason why I might not," Dan replied, eyes glowing with unmistakable mischief.

"What's that?" Torie couldn't help but ask.

"There aren't any eligible females."

"Why, England has several single females," Patty interjected, clearly puzzled.

Dan looked surprised. "Really?" He turned to Torie. "You told me you'd invite all you could find. Where are they?"

"Oh . . . um . . . none of them was available," Torie lied, blushing clear to her toes.

"None but you?" Louis quipped with a chuckle. Several guests snickered, and Torie saw more than one elbow being nudged and more than one wink being exchanged.

Mortified, she held onto her dignity with effort. "Get real. Dan and I are not the least bit interested in each other."

"That so?" her cousin retorted.

"That's *certainly* so," she told him, punctuating her words with a so-there nod intended to put an end to this foolish speculation once and for all.

"Then what the hell were the two of you doing at the pit last Wednesday at midnight?"

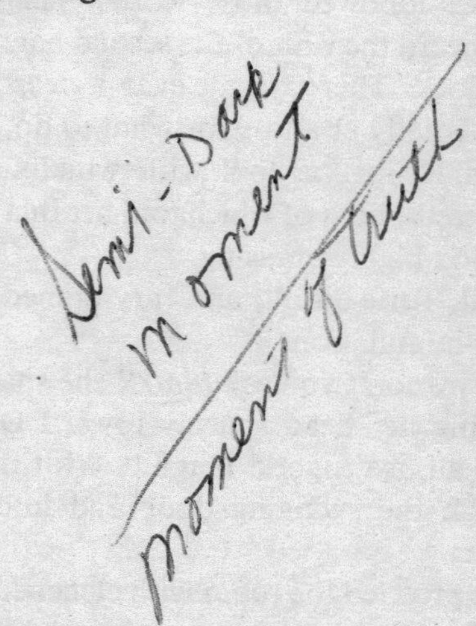

Chapter Seven

Silence followed those words—silence so intense that Torie heard the whir of the second hand as it moved on the wall clock. There wasn't even a peep from the kids next door. Totally at a loss for what to do, she risked a glance at Dan. He met her look with twinkling eyes and a flash of white teeth, both of which told her that he found the whole situation highly amusing.

Well, Torie didn't, and fury immediately got the better of her humiliation.

"Why don't you ask *him?*" she snapped to her cousin, inclining her head sharply toward Dan. "I'm sure you could all use a good laugh." With that, Torie sashayed through the swinging door and into the haven of the kitchen.

She prowled the room with clenched fists for a full minute afterward, trying to get control of her roller-coaster emotions. She wanted to scream; she wanted to cry; she wanted to kill . . . and definitely would, when she got Dan alone.

Opportunity presented itself almost immediately. Dan burst into the kitchen, cloaked in the sounds of raucous laughter from the other room. The door swung shut behind him.

"You okay?" he asked with a grin, blocking her path.

"Go jump in a lake," she replied coldly, pushing him out of her way. "Specifically, the pit!" She stalked to the refrigerator and swung open the door. With shaking hands, she retrieved a canned cola and then opened it to take a fortifying gulp. The bubbly liquid stung her throat, and coughing, Torie slammed it down on the counter. Dan was beside her in an instant, pounding her back as though he actually cared if she choked to death. "Leave me alone!"

He stepped back, hands up as though to ward off a blow. "All right, all right. Don't get your dander up."

"Don't get my...? Of all the nerve!" she exploded. "My reputation is ruined and all you can say is 'Don't get your dander up'?"

"For crying out loud," Dan retorted. "Your reputation is not ruined. Every single person in that room is married. They know all about the birds and bees. I'll bet three-fourths of them have made it in a parked car at the pit."

"And that's exactly what they think we did, too," she yelled.

Dan winced and clamped his hand over her mouth. "Shh. Do you want your guests to hear you?"

Thoroughly exasperated, Torie promptly bit him. He yelped and jerked back his hand. "*Now* you're worried about what they think?" She rolled her eyes heavenward and began to pace the room once more. "This is the worst thing that has ever happened to me. I'll never be able to look any of my friends in the eye again."

"Torie, honey, you're overreacting," Dan said, watching her warily from a safe distance.

"That's easy for you to say," she countered, halting her march to whirl and stomp back over to him. "Everyone thinks you're some kind of super stud. They think *I'm* easy."

"That's not true," Dan argued, clearly surprised by her vehemence.

"Oh? Then tell me what *is* true. What do they think I am?"

"The same woman you've always been—a woman they care about, a woman who's fully grown and entitled to live and love as she pleases."

"Love has nothing to do with this!" Torie exclaimed. "And don't you dare pretend that it does." She tossed back her hair over her shoulders and sighed heavily. "What a mess. And the heck of it is, the more I try to make it right, the worse it'll get. They'll never believe we're not having an affair."

"In that case, why don't we just have one?"

It took a full second for his astounding proposition to sink in. "Are you insane?" Torie blurted, taking a giant step back, her eyes big as cupcakes.

"No, I'm brilliant." He smiled. "The way I see it—we're damned if we do and damned if we don't. So let's do."

"You *are* insane."

"But it's the perfect solution," Dan argued. "To this problem and our other one."

"We have another problem?" she squeaked. This one was surely bad enough.

"Of course we do—the house."

"Oh, *that*. Forget the house. It's all yours. I've given it up, once and for all."

"But there's no need. We can share it."

"Share it?" Torie blurted in horror. "You mean you want me to *move in* with you?"

"Exactly. What do you say?"

"I say when hell freezes over," she told him. "I'd never, ever do such a thing. Why that's...that's...*degenerate*."

"But what about Wednesday night?" he asked, frowning at her.

"Wednesday night is one thing. Moving in with you, quite another. You bought that house so you could live in it. Now you can just do it."

Dan stared at her in silence for a moment, eyes narrowed thoughtfully. "I see," he finally murmured. "Now that you've given up on the house, you're not interested in fooling around with the owner anymore."

Torie tensed, not quite believing her ears or the insult. "And what's that supposed to mean?"

"It means that I caught onto your little scheme long before you admitted to it in the restaurant Wednesday night."

"Scheme? What scheme? What are you talking about?"

Dan laughed shortly. "You should get an Oscar for this one, honey. What scheme, indeed?"

His meaning slowly sank in. Torie swallowed hard and took a deep, fortifying breath. "Does that...? Do you...? Oh, God, I don't believe this. Are you actually insinuating that I'd *make love* with you to get your house?"

"No," he replied, his eyes now gleaming with something besides amusement. "I'm stating it flat out. You've been using me ever since you found out I bought the house, Torie Hanover. And now that you've finally realized that I'm not going to sell it to you, you're suddenly Miss Morals."

She gasped at the insult and clutched the counter to lend support to her shell-shocked knees. So he thought she was the kind of woman who'd use sex as a bribe. Worse, he'd been planning to take her up on the offer, knowing full well he had no intentions of selling the house.

Clearly he was not the man she thought him to be. Not only did he have no scruples, he was just like that truck he drove—a lobo, a wolf. Always on the prowl, Dan took what he could get and gave nothing in return.

And to think she'd wondered if he might be seeking hearth and home. At once as angry as she was hurt, Torie opened her mouth to lambaste him, but the words were never uttered. At that moment, the door swung open and Patty stuck her head inside.

"Everything okay in here?" she asked softly, glancing from one to the other of them.

"Just dandy," Torie snapped, swishing past her and into the dining room.

The last half of the party was a blur of good-natured jibes and teasing laughter. Dan went through the motions automatically. Though he mingled with his new friends and said all the right things, his heart was no longer in the fun. Something had gone wrong in the kitchen—terribly wrong—and he was only just beginning to figure out what.

From across the room, he watched Torie, much as he had all evening. She still chatted with her guests, but the animation had left her face. Her eyes no longer sparkled. She no longer laughed. Their gazes no longer met and mated.

He'd made a mistake—a big mistake.

Torie's shock and confusion at his allegations had been real, not the act he'd thought them to be. That meant something besides desire for his house had spurred her passion for him Wednesday night. Could it possibly be desire for its owner? he wondered. Did she actually want Dan Stewart, not for his possessions but for himself?

Maybe *then,* he decided, suddenly sick at heart. Certainly not now. She was obviously angry and hurt. She was also cool as an Arctic winter. He felt her chill clear across the room.

Cursing his stupidity for ever opening his big mouth, Dan spent the last moments of the party trying to corner Torie so he could explain and apologize. She steadfastly avoided him, however, and made certain they were never alone for a moment.

Around eleven-thirty, most of the guests rounded up their children and left. Since the few couples who remained were the ones Dan had asked to stay, Torie saw no reason to hang around. Instead, she made short work of cleanup and then tossed the keys to Louis, with orders to lock the door when they finished.

Dan's gaze followed her when she left the café. Deliberately she ignored it, just as she had his every attempt to talk to her. She'd heard enough out of him already and had no intention of listening to any more of his insults.

Getting close to Dan had been the biggest mistake of her life. And though he was right about one thing—a yearning for his house *had* prompted her initial friendliness—another emotion altogether spurred her passion in his arms. That was why his accusations hurt so badly. And because they hurt, she suspected the worst had happened.

In spite of every claim to the contrary, it looked as though she might be halfway in love with Dan Stewart, a man who considered her grasping and immoral. To make matters worse, he was a diehard bachelor, a rolling stone with no desire to gather that proverbial moss in the form of a wife and children.

After years of saving herself for a man who would appreciate and share her simple dreams, Torie had somehow done the incomprehensible, the unforgivable. She'd as good as given her heart to a gypsy.

And all she could do now was avoid him, so he wouldn't find out. He was, after all, a man without honor, a man who would use and abuse her love.

Therefore, she had no choice but to hide it from him.

Dan finally got away from the café at a quarter after one. Although he should have been thrilled that he finally had a painter, a roofer and a carpenter lined up, he felt only distress and intense regret for what had happened between him and Torie that night.

The depth of those emotions surprised him. He'd never wanted anything more than sex from her, after all. His heart wasn't involved.

Was it?

No, he told himself, as he drove home. He'd unwittingly hurt the feelings of a friend and he wanted to make things right. That, and that alone, was the reason he now sped to the trailer park they shared, fully intent on waking her and apologizing.

But Torie wouldn't come to the door.

Certain she was inside the house, most likely still in a temper, Dan gave in to his frustration and abandoned the soft-knock approach to pound on the door in earnest. When that didn't work, he called Torie's name so loudly that Jack Porter turned on his front-porch light.

And still she didn't respond.

"I know you're in there, Torie," Dan said. "And I'm not leaving until you come out here and talk with me."

Dead silence followed his threat.

"Five minutes," he pleaded, slapping his flattened palm on the door in his agitation. "Is that asking too much?"

"Way too much, since we have nothing to say to one another." Torie's words, filtering softly through the screen of the open window to the right of the door, caught Dan by surprise. He stood in stunned silence for a heartbeat before he found enough wits to step over it and peer inside. The closed curtains hid Torie from view, but, calmer now, Dan felt her nearness . . . and her desire.

"Actually, I have plenty to say," he told her quietly.

"I don't want to hear it."

"But Torie—"

"*I don't want to hear it*. Now go away . . . *please*."

Dan opened his mouth to argue, then shut it again. She was obviously in no mood to listen to what he had to say. Squaring his shoulders, Dan turned to head for home only to halt abruptly when he spied Jack, now standing outside in his boxer shorts. Dan winced, flushed and mustered what dignity he could by nodding a brisk good-night as he finished his trek and stepped through his door.

Once there, he looked at his watch, noting it was nearly two. He had to be in Charlotte by nine tomorrow. That meant he would have to leave England by 4:30 a.m. at the latest—much too early to wake Torie with an explanation she didn't want to hear.

It looked as though he had no choice but to direct his thoughts to his impending race. He owed his pit crew and his sponsor one-hundred percent of his concentration.

Whether he liked it or not, at the moment that responsibility took precedence over the apology he owed Torie.

Torie began Saturday as she'd begun every day since she met Dan Stewart. She crawled out of her bed and peeked out the bedroom window to see if his truck was home. This day, she discovered his vehicle was gone, and along with it, his RV.

Though she should have felt relief, Torie felt nothing but sadness and a tremendous sense of loss. She sampled those feelings deliberately, knowing that if she'd fallen in love with Dan and become involved with him, she'd have experienced them each and every time he left for a race.

That proved she was not cut out to love a gypsy, much less wed one. She needed the warmth of home fires, not camp fires. And now that Dan was out of her sight, maybe she could get him out of her heart, as well.

It wouldn't be easy, of course. Torie ached at the very thought of never kissing him again or experiencing the thrill of his touch. It had taken willpower she didn't know she possessed to turn him away in the wee hours of the morning. Only her fear that Dan might repeat his insulting offer had stopped her. Angry as she was with the man, she still didn't trust herself to resist him a second time.

She was like an addict, craving what she knew would hurt her. Only a cold-turkey cure—this week without him—would break her of the habit.

And with luck, this week would be enough time for her to undo whatever damage had been done to her reputation at the party. She could only hope it wasn't as extensive as she feared it to be.

On Monday Torie drove past Dan's house, as usual, on the way out of town. A disinterested glance—it belonged to someone else, after all—revealed that the structure looked the same as always—sadly neglected, distressingly empty.

When Torie returned to England that afternoon at six and repeated her ritual, she almost ran her car off the road. The entire front of Dan's house had been painted, the beginning of its transformation into the sunshine dwelling of her dreams. Though what she could see of the sides of the structure were still a weathered gray, Torie could easily envision how charming it would look when completed.

Her heart twisted.

What a waste, she thought. What a waste.

That night she did little more than watch television, deliberately avoiding the sports network that might offer a feature on race cars or the daring men who drove them.

As always on Tuesdays, Torie's classes were in England. She danced her way through the morning, then headed to the Eatery to pick up a bite to eat.

"Hello, there," her mother called, when she entered the café. "What do you hear from Dan?"

"I'm just fine, thank you," Torie caustically replied. "And how are *you?*"

Her mother laughed. "Sorry, sugar. How *are* you today?"

"I have a headache and my feet are killing me," Torie said.

"That's nice. Has Dan called?"

Torie huffed her exasperation. "No, Dan hasn't called, and why should he?"

"I just thought—"

"You thought wrong. Contrary to what everyone in this stupid hick town believes, we are not an item. Now what's the soup for today?"

"Chicken," her mother replied. "Shall I get you some? Surely if it can cure a cold, it can do *something* for that temper of yours."

"Sorry," Torie told her with a lusty sigh. "I didn't mean to snap at you. I guess I'm a little stressed."

"And no wonder. This is Dan's next-to-last race, after all, and he's got a darn good chance to win the Winston Cup again this year."

"Mo-ther!"

"Shall I fix it to go?"

"I think it would be better for all concerned."

A few minutes later, sack in hand, Torie exited the café. Without hesitation, she hopped into her car and went for a drive . . . that naturally took her right past Dan's house. No more painting had been done—that was a late-afternoon and evening task—but the roofing was about a third finished. Since Torie didn't see any signs of Jerry or anyone else, she assumed he'd gone home for lunch and so slowed to a crawl to get a better look at the place.

Too late, she spotted her best friend's husband sitting on the grass under the oak tree and waving her over. She stopped, backed and turned into the drive with reluctance.

"Whatcha up to?" Jerry called as he stood up and approached her, dusting off his backside.

"Not much, at all," she replied, getting out of the car. She leaned against it and glanced toward the house. "Looks really nice, doesn't it?"

"Shaping right up," he agreed with a nod. "Louis will probably finish painting the west end this evening. Red's supposed to have the Sheetrock and ceiling tiles delivered tomorrow morning, the flooring tomorrow afternoon." He grinned and tugged self-consciously on an ear in response to Torie's questioning look. "I volunteered to oversee things for Dan while he's gone. And speaking of Dan . . . what do you hear from him?"

Torie gritted her teeth at the inquiry. So they were a pair in Jerry's mind, too.

"Nothing," she snapped. "Why would he call me?"

"Damned if I know," Jerry replied with a grin and a shrug. "He's got enough problems on his hands without adding a sassy blonde."

"For your information, I'm not 'on his hands.' We're just good friends. And to assume for one instant that we are more is absolutely ridiculous."

"Right," Jerry drawled, eyes twinkling.

"You don't believe me, do you?" Torie demanded in exasperation, tossing her hair back.

"Sure I do. I swear."

Anxiously Torie read his expression, relaxing somewhat when he met her stare unflinchingly. "Thanks, Jerry. You're a good friend, too."

"Hot damn. Does that mean *I* get to watch the submarine races with you?"

"Arrghh!" Torie exclaimed, grabbing for his muscled neck with both hands.

Moments later, perhaps to save that same neck, Jerry promised not only to believe Tory, but to help convince everyone else that she and Dan were not a duo. As a result of that promise, Torie returned to her studio feeling much better. If she could get this very doubtful human being to believe her, then surely there was hope for the rest of the town.

Or maybe things weren't even as bad as she'd originally thought. Maybe everyone wasn't assuming the worst. Maybe no one but Friday's guests knew about the pit, and *maybe* they'd all kept their mouths shut.

Torie's brighter mood prevailed until Wednesday morning when she stepped out her front door and headed for her car for a day's worth of dance and exercise in Rush.

"'Morning," Jack Porter called from his front porch. Torie looked his way in surprise. She hadn't realized her antisocial neighbor rose as early as he went to bed.

"Good morning," she called back, smiling.

"What do you hear from your feller?"

Feller? *Feller?* Torie's smile vanished. Her face flamed, as did her temper. With difficulty she held it in check. "Who?"

Jack pointed to the parking spot Dan had vacated Saturday morning. "Him."

"He's not my fellow," Torie told him with an injured sniff.

"That so?" Jack replied, rubbing his whiskered chin. He shook his head slowly from side to side. "Could've swore it was you two they were talking about at the gas station yesterday."

The gas station? Torie looked around for a hole to crawl into. There wasn't one. "What exactly did you hear at the gas station?"

He scratched his head, frowning as though in deep thought. "I heard that some race-car driver and a dance teacher were surprised up at the pit one night last week."

Oh, God. "What a coincidence," Torie murmured with a light laugh.

"Is, isn't it?" He nodded solemnly.

"Is that all you heard?"

Jack pulled on his ear, again lost in his musing. "Naw. I also heard this here race-car driver and dance teacher were really fogging up the windows of that big ol' truck of his."

"They were not!" Torie exploded in mortification.

Jack grinned his delight. "They weren't?"

"No," Torie told him. "And I'd appreciate it if you'd set everyone straight on that, as soon as possible."

"Oh, I will," he said. "I surely will."

With that Torie got into her car and slammed the door. Muttering every expletive she knew, plus the ones she'd recently learned from Dan, she backed up the vehicle and left the tiny trailer park far behind.

Her day went downhill from there, and by that afternoon Torie felt no surprise at all when the mother of one of her Rush dance students asked if she was really dating the hunk from the truck commercials. With a laugh and a joke, Torie denied the rumor. And with a very heavy heart she returned to England shortly after.

If Torie could have avoided driving past Dan's house that evening, she would have. She was certainly in no mood to view restoration progress. Short of a nearly impassable back road, however, there was no other way into town, and try as she might, Torie could not pass by the house without looking at it.

A quick glanced revealed that the roofing was complete, as was the painting of the east end. The boards and Sheetrock remnants scattered all about the yard told Torie that interior work was underway, as well. In another couple of weeks, Dan would finish his racing season, do those commercials he'd told her about and move into the house . . . alone.

Torie tried to picture her life once Dan was settled. She imagined herself watching his comings and goings from a distance and without playing a part in them. Regret washed over her, a new kind that had nothing to do with the house and everything to do with the lonely ache she felt deep inside.

She realized with a start that she missed Dan—really missed him—and at that moment would have traded all the good reputation in the world for one of those phone calls everyone expected her to get.

But it never came, and once again she planned her night by the television schedule.

Thursday passed as uneventfully—and lonely—as the rest of the week. Torie rose, ate, drove to Faulkner, danced, ate, danced and drove back to England, exactly as she had for months. Dinner that evening consisted of toast with peanut butter, a meal that reminded her of Dan. Torie wasn't in the least surprised when her thoughts turned his way. Everything she'd done and seen that day had brought him to mind—from her breakfast of cookies and milk that morning to the afternoon view of his house, now sporting white gingerbread trim and green shutters.

As with every other night that interminably long week, Torie reached for the TV schedule when she finally settled herself in her rocker at eight o'clock. She scanned the list of programs for the evening, catching her breath when her gaze fell on the sports channel's Thursday night lineup. Without hesitation, Torie grabbed the remote control and turned on the little color set. Determinedly she flipped through the channels until she found the one she sought.

Eyes on the screen, bottom lip captured between her teeth, Torie leaned forward in her chair, anxiously watching the replay of the NASCAR time trials, which had taken place earlier that day. She saw many cars and many racers, few of whom she recognized . . . until the last fifteen minutes of the telecast.

Then . . . there he stood. Torie's heart leaped to her throat as her hungry eyes drank in the sight of Dan—so tall, so handsome, so dashing in his racing gear. He might as well have been in the room with her. The effect on Torie was the same.

"Oh, my," she softly breathed, pressing a hand to her suddenly fluttering heart. Dan looked every bit as formidable as the sleek machine behind him, and Torie wondered why the officials didn't just wave the checkered flag right then and there and cancel Sunday's race.

The way she saw it, the odds of anyone winning against him were just about the same as the odds of her forgetting him—slim, to none.

Entranced, Torie watched Dan's last-minute activities before he got into his car. As with years past, she found herself fascinated by every aspect of the sport, from the ultra efficient motions of the pit crew to the antics of the sportscaster, now waving a microphone under Dan's nose.

The camera moved in for a closeup, filling every millimeter of the screen with the familiar features of the face she loved. Torie let her gaze caress him from the tip of his nose to the top of his brow, all that was visible, since a safety helmet covered the rest. She discovered some new worry lines edging his eyes and decided he looked tired. Tired and maybe a little down.

Were things going badly in Charlotte? Torie suddenly wondered, frowning. Immediately she berated herself for her misguided concern. What did she care if he was having problems? He had insulted her, hurt her. And even if he apologized, she would not forgive him for what he'd believed.

Besides, Dan Stewart had made it clear that he wanted no woman worrying about him. He would not thank Torie for her efforts. They were opposites—two people better off without each other. They had different goals, incompatible goals. The sooner she put him out of her heart, the better off she would be.

But how was she going to do that? All her good intentions for this week without him had fallen by the wayside thus far, a very discouraging development. Torie was even more convinced she might be in love with Dan, and that in spite of the fact that she was still angry with him. It was definitely with waning enthusiasm that she clung to her determination to set the citizens of England straight about the two of them. This was probably because she really wished all the speculations were true. As annoying as it was to be considered half of the whole that was Dan, some secret part of her relished the honor.

Must be that darned nesting instinct of mine, Torie mused as she yanked the television plug from the wall outlet and banished Dan's sexy image of the airwaves. Handed down from mother to daughter since the beginning of time, that particular trait had turned countless houses into homes. Torie believed she'd inherited more than her fair share of it, the reason she could not, would not settle for less than full commitment from the man she loved.

And since Dan could not give her what she wanted, she would have to ignore her prevaricating feelings for him and continue her search for someone who could. Surely a forever-after, complete with wedding vows and children, waited for her somewhere out there. All she had to do was put Dan out of her mind so she could let this elusive someone else in.

To accomplish this, Torie decided, she would first have to put him out of everyone else's mind. As long as she and Dan were the object of so much speculation, the possibility of love and a committed relationship between them would be constantly in her thoughts.

So, renewing her determination to annihilate any and all rumors, Torie vowed once again to defend her honor. It was only Thursday, after all. She still had Friday, Saturday and Sunday to try to change the minds of England. With luck, she might even have a good part of Monday, too. Surely Dan would spend the night in Charlotte after his five-hundred-mile race. He was bound to be exhausted. In fact, now that she thought about it, he hadn't really said what he planned to do. Since he'd appointed Jerry to supervise the restoration of his house, he might just stay there for a while with his car and his crew or move on to Wilkesboro, the site of the final and most important race of the NASCAR circuit.

That meant he could possibly be gone from England another two weeks or maybe even longer . . . more than enough time to accomplish her goals.

And more than enough time to get over him.

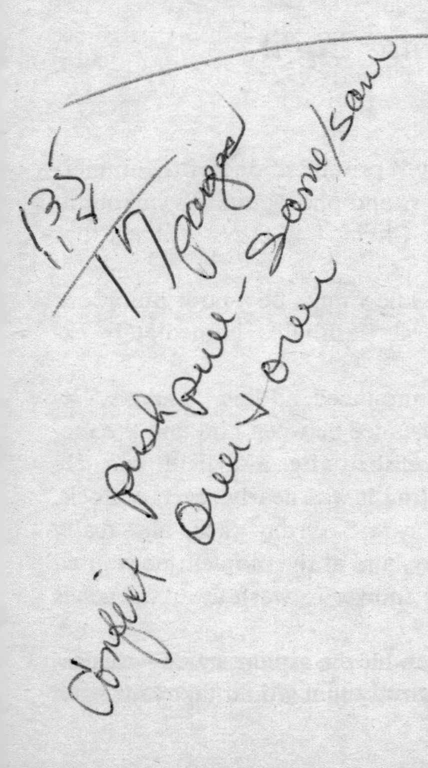

Chapter Eight

"You won, Danny boy," prompted one of the numerous reporters, sportscasters and photographers surrounding Dan in the Winner's Circle. "W-O-N. Where's that million-dollar smile?"

Dan mustered what he knew must be a poor imitation, then blinked when several flashbulbs immediately exploded.

"That's it, guys," he announced, adding "Thanks," as he stepped back to put distance between him and the media attention he usually relished after a difficult win. He glanced at his watch, noting it was nearly seven o'clock. The five-hour ordeal, a rare Saturday race, had really taken its toll on him today, and at the moment he wanted nothing more than a hot shower to wash away his aches and pains.

Then he fully intended to hit the asphalt again—this asphalt in the form of a highway that would take him back o England...to his house...to Torie. The past week away 'rom home had been pure hell.

That he already considered that little town and that old ıouse "home" was as amazing, Dan thought, as the fact hat he'd missed Torie so desperately. Time and again, he'd old himself that his gnawing need for her stemmed from exual desire or, perhaps, his determination to apologize.

He really knew better.

In spite of every determination to the contrary, it seemed hat he'd let Torie get under his skin. Somehow, without ven trying, she'd become as big an obsession as the racng. He could not put her out of his mind.

As a result, some long-buried dreams of hearth and ıome had gradually resurfaced over the past few days. And while Dan would not admit to being anywhere ready or the altar yet, he did acknowledge that he was prepared o offer more than just an apology when they stood face to ace once more.

He intended to offer himself. Again.

But this time, the proposition would be one Torie might ıctually consider. Based solely on the desire he believed hey shared, it would be free of the plots and counterplots vhich had nearly destroyed them before. He would preent his case earnestly and honestly. When he got through alking, Torie would know exactly what he would and vould not give her.

Dan could only hope that what he had to offer would be nough. He couldn't be sure, of course. Torie had her lreams—big dreams that she'd harbored since childhood ınd to which she was certainly entitled. And even though ıe'd once had similar goals and learned the hard way that hey were unrealistic, he had no right to ask her to compromise on hers.

Not that the compromise would be so very terrible. T Dan's way of thinking, he could be all she ever wanted…i she would settle for less than a forever-after commitmen that is. They could share a roof for as long as they wanted and with it, their lives, their laughter, their love . . .

Love? Dan smiled caustically to himself and headed fc the pits to gather his personal belongings.

Never love, never again, he thought as he walkec oblivious to the familiar sights and sounds of the race track, which he usually savored. Torie might have a hol on his body and soul, but she was still locked out of the no woman's land his heart had become. Dan sincerely be lieved that love would only complicate an otherwise per fect arrangement.

If he loved Torie, he would feel guilty every time he lef for a race. He would be distracted, miserable and lonel without her. If she loved him, she would grow to resent th sport and the time spent alone. She would unconsciousl begin anew her search for a man who would be there fc her twelve months of the year and perhaps give in t temptation when she found him. Bound by legal ties, the would struggle to hold onto promises that should neve have been made.

And humans that they were, they would surely fail.

Dan shuddered at the thought of such failure, knowin from experience what it could and *would* do to their lives He was too old for such heartache, and Torie was to young for it.

"What's up?" Pete Freeman, Dan's crew chief of seve years asked from just behind him, breaking into his trou bled thoughts.

"Nothing," Dan told him, flicking a glance his way. H saw his old friend's look of disbelief and sighed. "I'm jus a little tired, okay?"

"It *was* a hell of a race," Pete murmured. "But nothing an old pro like Dan Stewart can't handle." He arched a bushy eyebrow. "So what's eating you?"

"I said 'nothing!'" Dan snapped, halting his stride. He immediately regretted his uncharacteristic display of temper, knowing it wasn't the first one that week. "Hey, man. I'm sorry."

"Forget it," Pete said with an easy smile and a shrug. "Why don't you get cleaned up, rest for a while, and then come eat a bite with Amy and me?"

"Can't," Dan said, shaking his head. "I've got to hit the road. I'm going home tonight."

"You're going to Daytona?" Pete asked, clearly surprised.

"No. To England, Tennessee," Dan told him, adding, "Population—few. I've bought myself a house there, Pete."

The older man considered Dan's candid answer in silence for a second. "So that's where you were all last week. We wondered." He took off his cap and scratched his head. "Now what does a drifter like you want with a house?"

"I'm thirty-three years old," Dan said. "I can't travel the circuit forever. Besides, I can hole up there in the winters."

"But it's not winter now."

"No," Dan murmured softly, avoiding Pete's probing gaze.

"And I've never known you to stay away from your crew a whole week before, especially this late in the season."

Dan shrugged. "The house needs some work done on it, okay? I had a lot of arrangements to make."

"And that's why you're so distracted and miserable
Because you've bought yourself a place?"

Dan winced at the doubt in Pete's voice. Distracted an
miserable? Definitely. And when he added lonely to tha
he displayed all the symptoms of a man in love. Had Pet
somehow caught on to something Dan, himself, couldn'
own up to? "I, uh, want to see how it's coming along."

"Well, you can't go tonight," Pete told him. "We'r
supposed to meet Bern Dempsey for breakfast tomor
row."

"Damn!" the racer exploded, suddenly rememberin
the Sunday morning appointment he'd made with hi
sponsor's ad man. "I wonder if he could meet us tonigh
instead. That way I could pull out early tomorrow morn
ing."

"It's okay with me, if it's okay with him," Pete replied
He frowned. "You *are* planning to be at Wilkeboro for th
time trials next week, aren't you?"

Dan blinked his surprise at the question. "Have I eve
let you down before?"

"Noooo, but you haven't acted like this before, either."
Pete eyed him somberly. "You know, if I didn't know
better I'd say you've got more than a house waiting bac
in Tennessee. Have you gone and fallen for some littl
country gal?"

"Me? The Don Juan of the NASCAR circuit?"

Pete nodded at that. "Don Juan, hell. You haven't ha
a handful of dates since your divorce. And speaking o
which, how in the heck are you ever going to find some
one to share that new place of yours, if you don't go out?"

"I'm not looking for a housemate," Dan retorted
"And even if I was, I'd never find one. I don't have tim
to date, much less engage in a serious relationship."

"Where there's a will, there's a way," Pete quoted, proudly adding, "I'm living proof. Why, I met, courted *and* married Amy while I was traveling the circuit thirty-nine weeks of the year. Managed to father five kids, too."

"Amy could turn any man into a husband and any house—even one on wheels—into a home. She's special."

"And your lady's not?"

"My lady is very, *very* special," Dan blurted, not even realizing what he'd admitted until Pete grinned from ear to ear.

"Then I'll bet she could do it, too."

Dan flushed. "No. She'd never be able to cope with my life-style on a permanent basis. Trust me, I know."

"Don't judge all females by your ex, Danny boy."

"You think that's what I'm doing?"

"Yeah. And I'm not surprised. Cherry did a number on you, for sure."

Dan shook his head. "What are you talking about? That divorce wasn't her fault, it was mine. And if I'd been able to give up the racing when she'd asked me, we'd still be married today. God, she must have been lonely with me gone all the time."

"Lonely, my—" Pete broke off abruptly and cleared his throat. Standing in silence for a moment, as though in some kind of quandary, he readjusted the brim of his cap, then tugged at an ear, his gaze on the dispersing crowd in the grandstands several yards behind them.

"What's wrong?" Dan prompted, as always finely attuned to his old friend's moods. Clearly Pete had something on his mind, something he was reluctant to share.

"I, uh . . . what I mean is . . . aw, hell." Pete took a deep breath, glanced around as though to verify they were out of earshot of anyone, and tried again. "I may as well just tell you the truth. God knows it's past time for it. According to Amy, Cherry partied heartily every time you and I left for a race."

Stunned silence followed Pete's revelation. Not quite able to believe it, Dan studied his sober expression. "What are you saying to me?"

"I'm saying that woman didn't have a faithful bone in her body. Love may have made you blind, Dan, but some of us saw the truth. If Cherry asked you to choose between her and the racing, it was because she knew good and well what your choice would be. She wanted an easy out, and it's time you faced that fact, got rid of the guilt and started living again."

Another silence followed. "How come you never said anything about this before?" Dan finally asked, frowning at the trusted friend who'd acted as surrogate father for years.

"Believe me, I wanted to, but Amy said it would destroy you," Pete replied. "Frankly, I believe it's misbegotten guilt that's destroying you *and* your chances for happiness. That means it's time for the truth. I'm just sorry I had to be the one to tell you." Eyes downcast, Pete kicked at a nonexistent rock with his toe while his companion digested his words.

Dan stood in silence for a moment, his eyes on Pete's flushed face. "You know, I think I might take you up on your dinner offer, after all . . . if you don't think Amy will mind, that is. I have a couple of hundred questions to ask her."

Pete gulped. "About Cherry?"

"About Cherry."

Pete gulped again. "You *do* realize that Amy's going to figure out I've told you everything and guess why I did it. Females have an intuition about these things. Are you really ready for lectures on love, marriage and the race-track?"

Dan hesitated, thinking about the burden of guilt he'd carried for six years. He was more than ready to get rid of it—for a lot of reasons.

"I think I am," he murmured thoughtfully. "I really think I am."

The church was filled to capacity on Sunday morning, in spite of drenching autumn rains. Torie glanced back from her usual third-row-from-the-front, center-of-the-pew position, noting the familiar faces of family and friends, most of whom she had deliberately sought out and chatted with over the past two days.

More than one smiled or nodded a silent greeting, and turning her attention back to the front of the sanctuary, Torie sighed her satisfaction. Mission accomplished, she thought with a smug smile. All rumors about her and Dan had finally been laid to rest, and she'd made great leaps toward emotional recovery as a result.

It hadn't been easy; it hadn't been fun. But she'd done it, by golly, apparently convincing even her mother, who hadn't mentioned Dan's name once that morning. The final test would be later that day, of course, during and after Dan's race. If she could keep from plugging the TV set back in to watch it and if no one called to tell her how he'd done, she would consider herself victorious—over both the rumors and her wayward heart.

"A penny for your thoughts," Erma whispered from her right.

Torie started and glanced her mother's way. "They're really not worth that much."

"Oh, I don't know," Erma said. "You look like the cat that ate the canary."

Her daughter stifled an irreverent laugh. "I *am* feeling rather pleased with life today."

"That's a welcome change," Patty interjected from Torie's left, just as the choir began to sing the doxology that signaled the beginning of the worship service.

Refusing to relinquish her good mood, Torie ignored the comments and concentrated on the music. The stained-glass windows on either side of the room provided a glorious backdrop for the hymn of praise. And soon lost in the melody, Torie didn't notice the brisk draft that swirled around her feet, announcing the entrance of a latecomer, or the hush that fell on the congregation.

Torie's blissful ignorance of impending disaster did not last long, however, and suddenly conscious of something amiss, she tensed. Half turning to peer over her shoulder, Torie searched for the reason for her sudden premonition. Her gaze immediately collided with that of Dan's, who had entered the room and now stood at the back, apparently scanning the occupants, person by person, row by row. He winked when he saw Torie—winked and paraded straight down the aisle past seventeen pews of delighted parishioners.

When he reached her row, he stopped. Muttering an apology, he then crawled over the knees and legs of eight more of her fellow worshippers to wedge his six-foot-whatever frame into the nonexistent space between a snickering Patty and a horrified Torie, who barely choked back a shriek of sheer mortification.

"What are you doing here?" she hissed, when she could trust her voice.

"Church seems like a logical place to be on Sunday morning," he whispered back. Then he flashed that smile of his, the one she always felt clear to the bone. This time was no exception, and Torie almost melted in a puddle right there on the aged oak bench.

"For me, maybe," she retorted, clinging to her anger with great difficulty. It was so damn good to see him. Her heart rate would never be the same again. "You're supposed to be getting ready for your race."

"What race?" he asked, frowning.

"The race in Charlotte, you idiot."

"That was yesterday," he told her, adding, "I won," as he smiled again.

"Did a darn good job of it, too," Jerry interjected with a hoarse whisper from his spot on the other side of Patty.

"Thanks," Dan softly replied, just as the last refrains of the hymn died away.

Torie opened her mouth to let them both have it, but the words were never spoken since her mother elbowed her ribs rather sharply in warning. Swallowing back her temper, Torie planted her gaze on the preacher, now taking his place behind the massive pulpit.

She didn't hear a syllable of his usual welcoming speech . . . until he requested that everyone in the congregation stand and join hands with the friend next to him or her, while he led the opening prayer. Before Torie could stuff her hand into the pocket of her jacket, Dan grabbed it and laced his fingers with hers.

Short of making a scene, Torie could do nothing but fume in silence until the "amen" that would proclaim her freedom. But when it finally came, Dan wouldn't let her have her hand back.

Torie waited until they were seated again, then tried to tug free as surreptitiously as possible. They might as well have been bonded with glue for all that she accomplished. Huffing her frustration, she abruptly gave up and tucked their linked hands out of sight between them on the seat.

The moment she did that, she knew it was a mistake. The heat of his muscled thigh immediately penetrated her skin, traveling right up her arm and quickly spreading to encompass her entire body in a traitorously warm glow.

Darn the man, she thought, squirming. Again her mother elbowed her. Properly chastised, Torie risked a frown at Dan, who kept his eyes on the preacher, now deep in the sermon. She discovered a hint of a dimple she'd never noticed and realized Dan appeared to be enjoying her predicament. Well, he wouldn't enjoy it long.

At last the pastor gave the invitation and the choir sang the benediction. Relief washed over Torie when they finally stood for the closing prayer, hands still clasped.

Any moment, she thought, counting the seconds. Any moment.

"Amen."

Whew. Torie turned to Dan, fully intending to vent her frustration.

"Not here," Erma cautioned, as though she could read her daughter's mind.

Torie ignored her this time. "Let go of my hand, Dan."

"No."

"What?"

"Not until you agree to talk to me . . . in private. Let's take a drive."

"Forget it. I'm furious with you."

"I know," Dan said. "And you have every right to be. That's why I owe you an apology. Now let's get out of here so I can make it."

"If you apologized on bended knee, I wouldn't accept it," Torie said, once again trying to yank her hand free. Dan simply tightened his grip.

"And if *you* don't come with me right now, I'm going to embarrass you," he said.

Torie snorted her opinion of that ridiculous statement. "How could you possibly embarrass me more than you have already?" she demanded, trying with difficulty to ignore her mother, Patty, Jerry and everyone else who watched with avid interest.

"Would a great big hello kiss right on the mouth do the trick?"

Torie gasped her outrage. "Oh my G—"

"Torie!"

"—o-osh," she stammered, hearing her mom's warning just in time. Obviously she and Dan were going to have to finish this confrontation in private. There was no telling what he—or she herself might say or do. Shutting out the laughter of her friends and parent, Torie muscled her way past Dan and headed determinedly for the aisle and some much-needed fresh air. Of necessity—they were still attached, after all—he followed right on her heels.

Torie kept her eyes downcast as she led the way to the exit, too humiliated to face the folks she'd worked so hard to brainwash that week. Dan spoke to each and every one as though he'd known them for years, however, considerably slowing their escape.

"Will you just come on?" Torie hissed when he halted her yet again, this time less than a yard from freedom.

"Anxious to get me alone?" he teased, right in her ear.

"Yeah, so I can waste you," she replied, by now not caring who heard her.

Laughing, Dan nodded a goodbye to a rather startled couple and bundled Torie out the door. She snatched her umbrella from the rack as they exited, a wise move since torrential rains greeted them.

"Aw, man," Dan muttered, eyeing the storm blackened skies. "We're going to have to make a run for it."

"We're going in your truck?"

Dan nodded. "You can get your car later."

"Why don't I wait right here while you get the truck?" Torie suggested hopefully.

Dan merely laughed, not fooled for a moment. He took her umbrella in his free hand, opening it with the push of a button. "Ready?" he asked.

"Might as well be, I guess," she murmured with ill grace. Together they dashed for his vehicle, parked at the far end of the lot since he'd arrived late. Dan led Torie straight to the driver's side, and after letting go of her hand, helped her inside. She scooted over as far as she could, which was just about halfway since there was a large sack on the seat on the passenger side. Dan slipped behind the wheel, stashed the dripping umbrella on the floor mat beneath her feet, and inserted his key to start the engine.

"Where are we going?" Torie asked as he pulled out onto the highway.

"Coal Mountain."

"Whatever for?" Torie hadn't visited the theme park since it closed years ago, and she couldn't imagine why Dan would want to now that it was deserted.

"We need privacy and there's an old picnic pavilion there."

"*We're having a picnic?*"

"Uh-huh. Check out the sack."

Torie did, and was amazed to find bread, lunch meat, chips and soft drinks, all of which indicated that he'd planned ahead.

"When did you get back to town?" she demanded.

"A couple of hours ago." Dan glanced her way with a grin.

"How did you know where I was?"

"Jack Porter. He yelled out his window at me when I started over to your trailer right after I got mine hooked up."

"He would," Torie muttered under her breath.

"What'd you say?"

"Nothing."

Vastly irritated with everything—from Jack Porter to her traitorous heart, which had begun to race like crazy the moment Dan mentioned a private picnic—Torie glanced out the moisture-beaded window at the scenery.

So much for emotional recovery. One little smile had turned her brains to oatmeal, her morals to mush. Bewildered by her topsy-turvy feelings, Torie closed her eyes for a moment and mused on how different things would have been if Dan held down a normal job and she could let herself love him. With a mental sigh, she recalled an old nursery rhyme and tried to envision him as a doctor, a lawyer or an Indian chief. She couldn't, of course. Dan Stewart was a racer, through and through. His quest for speed was as much a part of him as his sense of humor, his turns of phrase, his smile. And it was the whole man who intrigued her, the whole man she desired.

That realized, Torie tried to imagine herself married to Dan the racer, traveling the circuit with him as she easily could until they had children and actually for several years after that. She had to admit that kind of life might be tolerable and even exciting if Dan shared it with her.

Home is where the heart is, after all, she reminded herself. And where was her heart? Dan's pocket, of course! That meant she should be happy anywhere, as long as he was within reach.

So now all she had to do was wrangle a proposal out of him to test her theory.

Proposal? From Dan Not-the-Marrying-Kind Stewart? Yeah. Right.

Swallowing back the laughter that suddenly threatened to bubble forth, Torie spied the turnoff to Coal Mountain just ahead. As Dan maneuvered the truck onto the narrow road, she marveled at how quickly she'd forgotten her anger and frustration with this man, not to mention the dreams of a lifetime. Proposal, indeed. As if she'd accept one if he gave it to her.

"So you won your race," she blurted, as much to break the heavy silence as to divert her train of thought from its crash course to destruction.

"My...? Oh. Yeah."

"I should think you'd be excited," Torie commented, eyeing his solemn face. He didn't look like a man one win away from his second Winston Cup.

"Oh, I am, I am. It was a damn difficult race but a good one." He shifted his gaze from the road to Torie and gave her a long, speculative look. "Too bad you missed it."

"I thought it was today," she blurted without thought.

"You mean you'd planned on watching it?" Torie heard the pleased surprise in his voice, saw his face brighten.

"I—um..." For some reason reluctant to hurt his feelings, Torie had to force herself to be candid. "Actually, no. I wasn't going to watch it."

"Oh." His face fell.

"My television set isn't working." That half truth, which had fallen so easily from her normally honest lips, shocked Torie to the core. What did she care if Dan thought she wasn't interested in his stupid old race?

"That's too bad. Want me to take a look at it later?"

"No need. I'll take care of it." Now thoroughly disgusted with herself for her weakness where Dan was concerned, Torie glanced over to him. She noted his windblown hair, his tawny eyes, his oh-so-kissable lips and knew in a flash why she couldn't seem to think straight when he was anywhere around.

The man was magic, and she'd fallen under his spell.

At that moment, Dan halted the truck a scant yard from one of the picnic pavilions rimming the once-famous park. He killed the engine and reached over Torie for the grocery sack, a move that put his face inches from hers for a second and took her breath away for several more.

Magic? Ha. Lethal was actually a better description of his effect on her wits and morals.

Once Torie got control of her lungs again, she followed Dan's lead, slipping out of the truck and ducking under the curtain of rain cascading off the roof that sheltered the single table and the man now standing next to it.

When she joined him there, he reached out to brush the droplets of water from her hair. His hand lingered a second more than necessary, and as intensely aware of him as always, Torie thanked her lucky stars that no marriage proposal would be forthcoming any time soon.

In her present state of confusion, she'd probably just accept it.

"So here we are," Torie said brightly, trying to get her mind off the wedding and forever after that would never be. She plopped down on one of the long benches attached to either side of the picnic table and then rested her back on the table itself. Crossing her arms across her chest, she demanded, "What now?"

"This," Dan said, dropping to one knee before her.

Chapter Nine

Torie's heart leaped right into her throat. Nearly choking on it, she sputtered, "W-what are you doing?"

"Apologizing," Dan told her. His eyes swept her flushed face. "What did you think I was doing?"

"Would you believe *proposing?*" she admitted with a self-conscious laugh.

Dan blinked his surprise, then laughed, too—hearty laughter that seemed to indicate he thought the idea as ridiculous as Torie did. He rose and sat inches from her on the bench, his arm resting on the table right behind her shoulders as he stared out at the rain beyond their cozy shelter.

"Just for the sake of curiosity," he said after a rather lengthy silence, "what would you have answered, if I *had* proposed?"

"What do you think?" she blurted in astonishment at the outrageous question. "We don't even love each other."

"We don't?"

Torie turned to face him, thoroughly baffled. "Of course we don't."

"Oh."

Something in that single syllable clutched at Torie's heart. She studied Dan's solemn expression, unable to decipher it. "You mean you thought we did?"

"No..." He stretched his legs out in front of him, crossing them at the ankle. "I knew we didn't."

Torie let out her pent-up breath. "Well, I'm glad we got that straight," she commented, relaxing against the table and his arm again. To her dismay, Dan raised his hand, absently stroking her hair.

"Is that the only reason you'd have refused me?"

Torie huffed her exasperation with their crazy dialogue and glared at him. "Why on earth do you ask?"

"Still curious," he told her. "Humor me."

"In that case, no," she replied after a moment's hesitation. "There are certainly others." Since not one of them came to mind at the moment, she could only hope his curiosity was satisfied.

Unfortunately it wasn't.

"Such as?" His fingers tangled in her curls. He shifted slightly, closing the distance between their bodies.

"Umm..." Well, darn. Frantically Torie searched through her brain for the reasons, which were apparently deeply buried under some recently hatched, oh-so-foolish fantasies of a forever-after with an auto racer. "I want a man I can depend on."

"I'll have you know I'm *very* dependable," Dan remarked, neutralizing the statement with a not-that-it-matters shrug. "I've never missed a race—as a member of the pit crew or as a driver."

"Which reminds me of the main reason I could never marry you," Torie said, coming abruptly to her senses.

"I've got my heart set on a man who'll be around summer, winter, autumn and spring . . . remember?"

"I remember," he said, so close his breath fanned her hair. "And just for the sake of argument, I have to tell you that could actually be arranged. My RV would be perfect for two."

"You know that's not what I meant."

"But there are a lot of wives traveling the circuits."

"Do they have children? I'd want a houseful myself, Dan. How would they go to school?"

"Amy Freeman, my crew chief's wife, told me that one of the drivers is married to a teacher who holds classes in her trailer during racing season."

"You talked to your crew chief's wife about this?" Torie gasped, floored by the unexpected revelation.

"Actually," Dan hastened to explain, "*she* talked to *me.* And since I was sitting at her table eating her pot roast, I had no choice but to listen."

"I . . . see," Torie murmured, oddly disappointed and totally disgusted with herself for feeling that way. "Well, while home schooling is a viable possibility, it's hardly ideal. Think of all that those kids must miss—the plays, the picnics, the friendships."

"And think of what they experience—the travel, the excitement, the—" Dan broke off abruptly and gave her a sheepish grin. "Not that it matters. At least to the two of us. I'm just trying to make you see that if you keep an open mind, there are workable solutions to most problems parents encounter while traveling the circuit."

"I realize that," Torie murmured, deliberately not adding her own just-formulated theory that once an offspring of theirs reached school age she would probably be secure enough in their relationship to let Dan leave her...as long as he called every night and came home as often as he could, that is. Even her own precious dad had his time away from the family. He had hunted and fished every chance he got and had been known to disappear for weeks at a time during deer season.

But turning a house into a home was a challenge not every woman could handle, and their particular circumstances only made things more difficult. Torie simply didn't know if she was willing or even able to stake her happiness on the off chance that she had what it took to do it.

She also didn't know why she was sitting with *this* man having *this* conversation.

"So you agree the problem isn't an insurmountable one?" To her annoyance, Dan sounded almost hopeful about their hypothetical nonsense.

"It doesn't make any difference whether I agree or not," Torie snapped, suddenly exasperated with the whole exchange. "The point is moot. We're not getting married. *We don't love each other.* Now could we please change the subject?"

"Suits me," Dan easily agreed. To Torie's surprise, he then placed a quick kiss on her temple. "I certainly didn't come here to propose—marriage, at least. I came so I could apologize and make you another kind of offer. One I'm hoping you won't be able to refuse."

"Oh, yeah?"

"Yeah. But first, I have to tell you how much I've missed you. This week away was surely the longest in my life."

"It was for me, too," she admitted.

Dan grinned his delight. "That's good to hear. And I believe it's a sign that we care for each other a great deal, even if we're not in love."

"It's certainly a sign of something," she agreed, not re sisting when Dan cupped her chin with his fingers an turned her to face him. His tender kiss seared her soul adding fuel to the fire already raging deep inside.

With a sigh, Torie melted into his embrace and slippe her arms around his waist. She matched him kiss for hun gry kiss, venting a week's worth of unrequited desire an intense loneliness.

As always each and every touch fanned the flames o passion no amount of rain could extinguish, and it wa with reluctance she pulled away from this man she did no love and who did not love her back.

"I'm really sorry I accused you of trying to seduce th house from me," Dan murmured when she did. "I kno now you'd never do such a thing."

"Actually I did have an ulterior motive for hangin around . . . at first, anyway," Torie replied. "That wasn' the reason for what happened between us at the pit though."

Dan smiled into her hair. "And what was the reason fo that?"

"Lust, pure and simple."

Dan groaned. "We could be back there in fifteen min utes flat. Want to go?"

"And risk the humiliation of getting caught again? No on your life."

Dan released her at that and got to his feet. He walke to the edge of the cement floor and looked out into the rai still falling in torrents. Torie joined him almost immedi ately. Wrapping her arms around his waist, she hugged hin hard from behind and buried her face in the rough yarn o his sweater.

He said nothing, merely turning in her embrace unti they were face to face, when he dipped his head to kiss he briefly. Smiling tenderly, he murmured, "Now that I've finally gotten that apology out of the way, I'm ready to make the irresistible offer I mentioned."

"And what might that be?" Torie asked, curiosity piqued.

"I want to share the house with you."

"Hmm. Seem like I've heard this offer before."

"No, not this one. Another one, one made in the wrong spirit," Dan assured her. "And one for which I apologize."

"I see. And just why are you making this new and different offer?"

"For several reasons. To begin with, you have a claim to the house."

"Only a minor moral one."

"Minor moral ones count."

"Since when?" Torie demanded.

"Since I spent a week away from you," Dan answered. "Another good reason we should share the house is that it's much too big for one person. Why, I could put everything I own, including my truck and camper, in the den. What about the rest of those empty rooms?"

She smiled at his foolishness. "And the next reason?"

"I want you, Torie Hanover—under my roof, in my bed, throughout my life. Move in with me. You can keep your job and stay here alone while I'm gone, or you can give it up and travel the circuit with me, whichever you want to do. Hell, you can even try both, for that matter. We've got the rest of our lives to find a workable solution to this desire we have for each other."

Torie perused his earnest face, wishing the "workable solution" was really as attainable as he seemed to think. She knew it wasn't, however, knew he hadn't thought of all the pitfalls to such an arrangement. "I'm sorry, Dan. I just can't do it."

"Because of your reputation?" he asked, stepping away to watch the rain once more.

"What reputation?" she responded with a dry laugh. "As you pointed out to me before, we're damned if we do and damned if we don't...especially after today's little fiasco."

"So what's the problem?" Dan asked, turning back to her.

"Problem? *Problem?* There's a long list of problems, which I'll be glad to enumerate for you. Have a seat."

Frowning slightly, Dan did as she ordered.

"Number one is the house," Torie said, pacing to and fro in front of him. "I still want it as much as you do, you know, maybe even more, since I've lost it twice already. How can I move in, knowing that someday I might have to give it up, yet again, if we can't get along with each other?"

Dan winced, but didn't reply.

"Number two is my job. What if I *do* quit dancing and travel the circuit with you? And what if things don't work out between us? It took me a solid year to build up my clientele and set up my studio. Of necessity, I lived on a shoestring budget during that time. I'm not at all sure I'm willing to risk my hard-earned financial security for a relationship as iffy as ours."

"I'd help you get on your feet again, if we split," Dan told her.

"Even if we're on less than friendly terms?" Torie demanded, momentarily halting her march.

"We could work out the arrangements up front."

"A *pre-affair* agreement? Isn't that an admission of defeat before we even begin?"

Again Dan made no reply, but his stormy expression told her his opinion of the turn their conversation had taken.

"Number three," Torie said, pushing relentlessly on. "What if I do the unforgivable and fall in love with you somewhere along the way? What if you don't fall in love with me? What if you decide you'd rather have a dog as a companion, after all, and call the whole thing off? I'm quite sure I'm not up to that kind of heartache."

"I can say with complete assurance that will never happen," Dan said with a grin.

"You own a crystal ball, do you?"

"I don't need one. You're a dear friend, Torie. I care for you and I'd never do anything to hurt you. It's a lot more likely that you'll be the one to fly the coop."

Torie laughed at his ridiculous words but cautiously revealed nothing of the precarious state of her heart. "Which brings me to problem number four. What if we *both* fall in love? What if we decide we can survive together and actually marry?"

Dan groaned loudly at her question. "Are we back to *that?*"

"It could happen, Dan. Admit it."

"All right. I admit it. It could happen."

"And if we married, we might have kids. What if I gave up traveling with you and elected to stay home with them, which is really the only logical solution once they get to school age?"

"By then we'll be old pros," Dan exclaimed, his face brightening. "And all the glitches will already have been worked out of our relationship. It'll be smooth sailing forever."

"All the glitches?" Torie echoed incredulously, sitting down next to him, peering earnestly into his eyes. "Get real. Isn't it much more likely there'll be a whole new set of them?"

"For example?"

"It's one thing to say goodbye to a lover who has made no commitments and asked for none in return. It's quite another to say it to the father of my children, a man who has vowed to be there for richer or poorer, in sickness and in health. I could easily grow resentful of being stuck at home with a child, especially if I'd gotten used to being with you every hour of every day."

"I know it would be tough on you, but when the season ended, I would more than make it up."

"You probably would," Torie said. "But aren't you forgetting it isn't just me who'll be lonely when you hit the road? You'll be at loose ends, too. And if you think *this* week alone was bad, just wait until you've had me in your bed for a while."

Dan gulped audibly and closed his eyes, making no comment.

"And what about our children?" Torie persisted. "What if you're not there when our son wins first prize in the spelling bee? When our daughter recites her poem at the PTA meeting? Don't you realize what you could miss?"

"Hold everything!" he suddenly exclaimed, leaping to his feet, face flushed. "We've gotten offtrack here. Way offtrack. All I ever intended to do is share my house with you. Why are we talking love, weddings and—" he shuddered "—PTA?"

Torie bit back a laugh at his horrified expression. "Because I want you to face facts. If we move in together, we could be making the biggest mistake either of us ever made. Surely you can see that."

"*Now* I can," he grumbled. "And I'm wondering why I ever opened my big mouth. Sharing the house was obviously a dumb solution—an incredibly dumb solution—to our problem. Too bad it's the only one I had." With that, he grabbed Torie's hand and tugged her in the direction of the truck.

"Where are we going?" she asked, just before he dragged her into the rain.

Dan halted. "Home, of course. No reason to hang around here any longer." His expression suddenly brightened. "Unless you have a bright idea of your own?"

Torie shook her head. "I'm afraid not. I was just wondering about our picnic."

Dan slapped his palm to his forehead in remembrance. "I'm sorry. I forgot all about it. You're probably starved."

"And you're not?" Torie asked, swiveling around to face the sack and patting the seat next to her.

"Actually I seem to have lost my appetite," he grumbled, nonetheless maneuvering his long legs between the bench and the table so he could sit beside her.

"You'll change your mind once you've smelled the food," Torie promised, reaching for the sack. From it she extracted bread, bologna and mustard. Seconds later, she handed Dan a sandwich on a napkin. "Now eat. You'll feel better."

He stared at it unenthusiastically. "I can't do it."

"Does this mean I get to eat yours, too?" she joked, taking a big bite of her own sandwich.

Dan glared at her. His carefully thought out proposition had just washed away like dead leaves in a rain gutter, and all she could think about was food? "You're taking this whole thing rather lightly, aren't you?"

Torie stopped chewing and stared straight ahead. "God knows, I'm trying to." She swallowed hard, then opened her mouth for another bite. Instead of taking it, however, she laid the sandwich on a napkin and pushed it away. To Dan's horror a solitary tear snaked down her cheek and splashed onto her jacket.

"Don't do it," he groaned, a millisecond before she burst into tears and buried her face in her hands. Dan hesitated only a moment before he straddled the bench and tugged her into his arms, soothing her with whatever words came to mind. For what seemed an eternity, the storm inside the pavilion rivaled that outside it. Then Torie seemed to get control, calming herself to an occasional sniff and shudder.

Finally she eased free and gave him an apologetic smile. "Sorry about that. You'd think I had a broken heart or something."

Dan laughed shortly at her words. "You can't have a broken heart without love, and I think we've more than eliminated that possibility."

"So we have," she murmured with a wry laugh of her own. "And a lot of other ones, as well." She gave him a wan smile. "Thanks for the offer to share your house. I'm really sorry I can't take you up on it—the reason for the tears, I guess." At that, Torie wrapped both the sandwiches and stashed them in the sack. Then she stood away from the table. "Maybe it would be best if we just went on home."

"Yeah." Sick at heart, Dan finished cleaning up and then tucked the sack under his arm. Seconds later they were heading back to town, both silent and thoughtful.

Dan turned the truck into the parking lot of the church barely an hour after the two of them left it, but in an entirely different frame of mind. They sat without words when he stopped the vehicle, exchanging more than one wistful gaze before Torie finally reached for the door handle. Dan stopped her with an outstretched arm. "I was planning on hanging around until the weekend, but under the circumstances, maybe I'd better go ahead and leave town early."

"Don't do it on my account," Torie told him. "We're going to have to get used to running into each other every time we turn around. Little towns are like that, you know."

"Yeah," he murmured glumly, trying to picture himself meeting and greeting Torie without giving her a hello kiss. The sudden realization that there would be no more kisses—hello, goodbye or *whatever*—nearly got the best of him and for a fraction of a millisecond, Dan wondered if the racing was really worth it.

Stunned to his toes by the traitorous thought, he responded to Torie's soft goodbye with nothing more than a slow nod. Dazed, he watched her get into her car. Silent and regretful, he then followed her to the trailer park, where they parted without so much as a wave to each other and resumed their separate lives.

The next few days were the longest in Dan's life, easily outstretching the entire week spent alone in Charlotte. He saw Torie only once—at the eatery.

Dressed in her usual leotard, she held a similarly clad child, probably a student, who looked to be about two or so. Blond-haired, dark-eyed, the toddler stole Dan's heart the moment he laid eyes on her, and he couldn't help but think that a child of his and Torie's could easily have that striking coloring.

A child of his and Torie's? Fat chance.

Though Torie spoke cordially as she slipped past him, there was no sparkle in her eyes, no warmth in her smile. The fact that Erma fed Dan in stony silence only made him feel worse. And when she presented him with a slice of her famous peanut-butter pie, he actually managed to choke it down, knowing he should be darned grateful she hadn't served him arsenic, instead.

Several times that week, Dan decided he would be better off at the racetrack with his car and crew. He couldn't actually bring himself to leave England, however, a development he found amazing, since racing had been the focus of his life for nearly a decade and this race was the last and, therefore, the most important one of the year. Dan wondered briefly if his lack of enthusiasm might be a permanent condition and then tried not to think about it again, knowing that a win at Wilkesboro would be difficult enough without the added stress of divided loyalties.

Work on the house continued at a steady pace, and it gradually blossomed into a dwelling worthy of a spread in any home-and-garden magazine. Dan, who knew next to nothing about restoring old houses, arrived on the scene with the sun both Monday and Tuesday mornings and then spent the day lurking about, distracting the carpenter, electrician and plumber, all hard at work.

On Wednesday, he wised up—with a little help from his new friend Jerry Millsap—and stayed out from underfoot by spending most of his daylight hours at the gas station and the hardware store. Dan made new friends everywhere he went, and invariably found himself the object of very earnest advice to the lovelorn. Still relatively ignorant of the extent of the small-town grapevine, Dan was endlessly amazed that every one seemed to know all about his and Torie's troubles. By that afternoon, he'd definitely begun to understand why she'd gotten so upset when they were surprised at the pit.

Every evening after the workmen left and while there was still some daylight, he met Jerry Millsap at his house and together they made an inspection of what had been done. Thursday was no exception, and when Dan pulled into the drive, he spied Jerry on the porch. After saying their hellos, the two men headed inside the house. A quick walk-through revealed that it would probably be ready for occupancy in a couple more weeks, just about the time Dan returned from the ad promotion following his final race.

Though he should have been thrilled that the timing of his project was going to be so perfect, Dan actually felt little more than the same numbness that had gripped him all week. He did manage to thank Jerry for his managerial efforts and skill. It was good to have someone knowledgeable behind the scenes—here as well as on a racetrack. He wasn't too proud to admit it.

Jerry laughed off his words and led the way back outside. "Delighted to do it for you. Patty and I have been fans of yours for years. And speaking of which, when are you going to Wilkesboro?"

"I'm not sure. I really need to drop by and visit my mom in Knoxville before I go," Dan said as they stepped onto the porch. He noted that darkness had settled like a blanket over the house while they were indoors. "It's her birthday, and I've missed it the past four years. I'll head to the track after I take care of that, I guess."

"This is the big race, huh?" Jerry commented, rocking back on his heels, thumbs hooked in his belt loops.

"The big one," Dan echoed dully.

Jerry frowned, obviously picking up on his new friend's lack of enthusiasm. "You got a bad feeling about it?"

"About life in general, at the moment," Dan admitted, his mind on his lack of enthusiasm for not only the race but his house.

"Am I right in assuming that Torie Hanover has a little something to do with that?"

Dan didn't bother to play innocent. "You are."

Jerry shook his head and rolled his eyes. "Why don't you just give in and marry her, for Pete's sake?"

"It's not that simple."

"Maybe it should be. You can think too hard and long about things, you know. Sometimes it's best to go with your gut instinct and work out the details later."

Like I did when I bought the house? Dan suddenly wondered. That had certainly been an impulsive decision, yet one he hadn't regretted.

"For instance," Jerry went on, "if you wait to have kids until you can afford them, you'll leave this world without heirs. If you wait to get married until you work out all the problems, you'll die a bald-headed bachelor."

Bald-headed bachelor? Dan winced at what was not a pretty picture.

"The way I see it," Jerry then said, "marriage is a lot like racing five-hundred miles at top speed. The only sensible way to tackle that big a challenge is a lap at a time. Right?"

"Of course."

"Well, the only sensible way to tackle marriage and forever after is a day at a time."

A day at a time . . . a day at a time. Dan savored the surprisingly philosophical advice, desperately wanting to believe there was a chance for him and Torie. The man in him saw merit to Jerry's theories; the little boy saw a big chance for another heartache.

Never in his life had Dan been so confused. His head spun with it.

"So what are you going to do?" Jerry asked, breaking into Dan's troubled thoughts. He lay a hand on the racer's shoulder, peering intently at him through the dark.

Do? Dan almost laughed. Jerry actually thought he was ready to *do* something? Suddenly at his wit's end, Dan called a time out in his week's worth of confusion. "I'm going to drink an ice-cold root beer, that's what I'm going to do. Want to split a six pack with me?"

Jerry gaped at him, then burst into laughter. "Sounds like a winner to me," he said, slapping Dan on the back. "Let's get out of here."

"If one more person offers advice on how to get Dan back, I'm going to scream," Torie announced as she burst into the Eatery at seven-fifty-five that same night.

"What happened?" her wide-eyed mother asked. She handed Torie a soft drink and motioned her over to the counter she was wiping down.

Torie sat on a stool and heaved a sigh. "Well, I ran into Mary Shelton and the Widow Cline at the grocery store a while ago and spoke to them, just like I always do."

"And?"

"And Mary gave me her recipe for red velvet cake—the one that's been a family secret for years, mind you—and told me if I would bake it, I'd have Dan in my kitchen in no time flat."

Erma chuckled. "I've always heard that the way to a man's heart is through his stomach."

"Yeah, well, someone needs to tell the Widow Cline."

"Why? What was her advice?"

"She suggested that I wear a black lace teddy when I served it."

Erma howled with laughter at that, a sound Torie found vastly irritating.

"This isn't funny," Torie snapped, once her mother had mopped her eyes and gained a measure of control.

"Yes, it is. Don't let those two biddies steal your sense of humor."

"But it's not just them. I bumped into Susan Winters as I was leaving, and she asked me if it was true that Dan and I had broken up."

"What did you tell her?" Erma asked.

"I told her 'no,'" Torie said, lamely adding, "Which was true, since we weren't even going together in the first place."

Erma sobered immediately and joined her daughter at the counter. "Now was that fair to Dan?"

"I suppose not," Torie admitted. "But I just couldn't bear the thought of the two of them together."

"Why not? *You* don't want him."

"Oh, but I do."

"You do?"

"Of course, I do," Torie told her with a heartfelt sigh.

"Then what is the problem?" Erma demanded in exasperation.

"I'm scared."

"Scared of what?"

"I don't know."

Shaking her head in dismay, Erma sat in silence for a moment, then reached out to give her troubled daughter a hug. "Have I ever, in your twenty-two years, lied to you, steered you wrong, given you bad advice?"

"Yes," Torie replied.

"When?" Erma demanded, clearly surprised.

"When you told me that boys think braces are sexy."

Erma winced. "Besides that."

"I guess not."

"Then listen to your mother now. If you even *think* you love that man, you go after him. True love is a blessing not everyone receives. Never question it. Never fear it. *Always* hold onto it."

69
152
17
17 pages
Wants Him Bad

Chapter Ten

Dan paced in his trailer long after Jerry left that night, no nearer peace of mind than before the root beers and the lecture. Not that Jerry's words didn't make sense. They did . . . sort of . . . and at one point, Dan had actually admitted that marriage might be the answer, more to get his friend to shut up than for any other reason. Now, alone and in blessed silence, he knew better, of course. For that reason, he grabbed up his sleeping bag, a pillow and a clean shirt. Ducking the sprinkling midnight rain, he got into his truck and headed for his house. Dan felt certain that the key to his happiness lay hidden there. All he had to do was find it, thereby restoring the joy and satisfaction of those first moments as proud owner.

By the time Dan arrived at the dwelling, another autumn squall was in progress, this one complete with special effects in the form of rumbling thunder and brilliant lightning. Dan parked the truck as close as he could and dashed under the cover of the porch where he stood for a moment, watching the storm. Though violent, it was nothing compared to the emotional tempest that raged inside him.

The lightning flashed almost constantly, and since the electrician had not completed his wiring of the house, Dan took advantage of its brightness when he finally entered the empty structure and wandered slowly through it. He tried to imagine how the place would look once he had furniture in the rooms, drapes on the windows, pictures on the walls.

It would be cozy, he promised himself. It would be home.

Home?

Dan shook his head, knowing in his heart of hearts that it would take more than a couch or a curtain to turn this house into a home. It would take laughter. It would take tears. It would take love.

And it would take a wedding.

He'd made a mistake—a big mistake—in thinking he could live here alone and be content. Torie, not the house, was the key to his happiness. Without her, he would never be satisfied living there.

So now what? Dan asked himself, sinking down to sit on the stairs in the barren living room. Oblivious to his surroundings—dark one second, dazzling bright the next—he searched the deepest recesses of his heart for a solution to his dilemma. There weren't any easy ones, and only after much agonizing did two choices finally come to mind: he could give up the racing and maybe win Torie, or he could give up Torie and keep the racing.

To make the first choice, he would have to be committed heart, soul and mind. He would have to be head over heels in love. And therein lay the problem. Not only was

Dan confused about his own feelings, he was remarkably ignorant of Torie's.

With a sigh of dejection, Dan thought back to his earlier conversation with Jerry and his friend's comparison of marriage to auto racing. That parallel, logical as it sounded at the time, had nonetheless bothered Dan, and now he knew why.

Though he tackled his five-hundred-mile races a lap at a time, just as Jerry pointed out, he did it in a dependable car, with good tires and plenty of fuel. If he and Torie tried to tackle marriage, whether a day, an hour or even a second at a time, they would be doing it unprepared—without the two most important prerequisites: love and a willingness to compromise. They would not be able to survive the long haul; they would not win the race.

And that eliminated his first choice quite neatly. He would be nothing less than a fool to sacrifice his career for maybe love.

Heart-weary, Dan stood and made his way slowly to the master bedroom, aided only slightly by the lightning, which was now little more than an occasional ghostly glow. Once there, he wasted no time in ridding himself of his shoes and eased his tired bones into his sleeping bag. Closing his eyes, Dan prayed that the peace of a wise decision would come with the dawn.

But it didn't.

With the dawn came the clearheaded realization that though he had made the only possible choice he could make, there would be no peace...of heart or of mind...ever.

Sadly Dan accepted, once and for all, the inevitable and then faced the ramifications of his choice. Obviously there was no point in keeping the house. He would never be happy in it. That meant Jerry had been wrong all around.

Impulsive decisions were not good ones. Buying this place had been one of those decisions. Marrying Torie would be, too.

Dan slipped out of his shirt and dropped it on the sleeping bag, which he left in a tangled heap on the floor. After pulling on a fresh shirt and his shoes, he made one more walk through the house. His footsteps echoed hollowly through the house, and unable to bear the emptiness of the dwelling and his heart, Dan headed straight for the bathroom, where he made quick work of washing his face and combing his hair. Minutes later, he stepped out onto the porch.

He glanced at his watch, noting it was just after six. His workers would be there at any moment, as would Jerry. Dan didn't want to see any of them right now. He wasn't sure he could share his decision to sell the house without breaking down. He certainly wasn't up to any questions about it.

For that reason, he strode to his truck and got in. A twist of the key started the engine, and in seconds he was on the highway headed away from the dreams of a lifetime.

When Dan reached the trailer park, he turned into the drive and halted his truck in front of his RV. He stepped out of the vehicle and walked with determined steps to Torie's, fully intent on doing the only fair thing: offering the house to her. If there was any consolation to his decision to give up the property, it was his knowledge that Torie loved it every bit as much, if not more, than he did.

It took her several long minutes to answer his summons, and when she did, Dan very nearly lost sight of his mission. Long hair tumbled around her face and shoulders, Torie stared up at him through blue eyes wide with surprise. At once, all the other consequences of his painful decision hit him full in the heart.

Never would he kiss those lips again, or touch that silky hair. Never would he have her in his bed, looking just as she looked now right this moment—sleepy, sexy, so ready to love.

But there was no love, he reminded himself, steeling his heart against her.

"Dan! What are you doing here?" Torie demanded, clutching together the edges of a long chenille robe.

"I need to talk to you."

She stood in silence for a moment, then pulled open the door and stepped back.

"No. This won't take but a minute." He swallowed hard and then plunged ahead. "Do you still want the house?"

"Do I—" Torie broke off, clearly baffled by the unexpected question. "I, uh...guess so. I mean, yes, of course I want it."

"Then, it's yours. We won't be able to work out the details until I get back from the truck promotion in a couple of weeks, three tops. By then the workers should be finished, anyway."

"But what—"

"I really don't have time to explain right now," Dan interrupted. "I have to hit the road."

"But why—"

"We'll talk later."

"But Dan—"

"'Bye, Torie."

Lunging, she caught his arms to halt him. "What is going on?"

"Nothing," he said, half turning back to her. "I just changed my mind about it, okay?"

Torie scanned his face. "I don't understand."

"You don't have to," he told her, jerking his arm free. Again Dan moved to leave. Again she stopped him, this time by stepping outside to block his exit from the porch.

"But this doesn't make sense."

"It does to me. Now, I'll see you in a few weeks." *Maybe.* Right now he wasn't at all sure he'd ever be able to face her again. He hesitated for a moment, his gaze caressing her from head to toe, trying to memorize every detail. Then abruptly, he closed the distance between them, hugging her hard, pressing his lips to hers.

Dan's kiss was intense, frightening, and...final. And his next words did nothing to alleviate the sudden dread that clutched Torie's heart.

"Maybe, someday, we'll both find what we're looking for."

Weak as a kitten when he released her, Torie could only clutch the side railing and watch in stunned silence as he leaped off the porch and jogged to his RV. A millisecond later, he disappeared inside it.

Dazed, fingers pressed to her tingling lips, Torie turned and reentered her trailer. She walked straight to her bedroom and peered out her window, staring at Dan's truck and camper without really seeing them.

Something was wrong, terribly wrong. And until she knew what it was, she would not be able to enjoy this unexpected acquisition of the house. What could have happened to make Dan change his mind? she agonized. Why would he abandon so abruptly the dreams to which he'd clung for years?

Impulsively Torie shed her sleepwear and pulled on jeans and a sweatshirt, intent on confronting Dan to find out the truth. She brushed her hair with haphazard strokes, fastened it in a ponytail, then stepped into worn loafers. Dashing to the front door, Torie threw it open...just in time to see Dan drive off into the sunrise in his truck.

Stomach knotting with concern and confusion, Torie headed immediately for the phone. Gut instinct told Torie there was only one other person who might be able to shed a little light on Dan's astonishing behavior—Jerry Millsap. He and Dan had been buddies since they were introduced, and she intended to wrest the truth from him *now.*

But Jerry was not home, and according to Patty would not be until six-thirty or so that night and then had league bowling at seven in Faulkner. Further questioning revealed that Jerry was at Dan's house, supervising restoration. Vowing to talk to him when she finished her classes that afternoon, Torie hung up the phone and got on with her day.

The clock hands moved with tormenting slowness that Friday. Torie could not count the times she glanced at her watch and discovered only five or maybe ten minutes had passed since the last check. Finally her pupils said their goodbyes and she crawled wearily into her car.

Pushing the speed limit more than a little, Torie fairly flew back to England and the answers she hoped Jerry would have. It was a quarter after six when she arrived at the house, and the two familiar vehicles parked out front told her that only Jerry and the electrician remained.

As she pulled into the drive, the electrician stepped from the house. Nodding to her, he loaded a box into the back of his car and then got into it. A second later he left.

Torie scrambled out of her car immediately and hurried to the porch. Since the front door was open, she walked right on inside, calling out for Jerry as she entered the living room.

"Yo," he yelled from somewhere in the vicinity of the kitchen. Torie made a beeline in that direction and found

Jerry down on his hands and knees on the floor, peering under the kitchen sink. "This darn pipe is still leaking. I guess I'd better call the plumber tonight." Ducking out from under the cabinet, he stood, swiped his hands down his jeans and grinned mischievously at Torie. "Sooo, what brings you here? Come by to make sure Dan's done everything to suit you?"

"Then you know he's decided to sell the house to me."

"What?" Jerry's eyes rounded, and all traces of amusement vanished.

So he *didn't* know, after all. Torie's spirits sank to a new low. "I take it you're as surprised as I am?"

"Hell, yeah, I'm surprised. Why, last night he said—" Abruptly Jerry broke off.

"He said what?" Torie prompted eagerly.

"I, uh . . . nothing. He said nothing."

"You're lying to me, Jerry."

"I swear the man said nothing about giving up the house."

"Then why is he doing it?" Torie demanded. "What has happened?"

"Damned if I know," Jerry muttered, frowning. "I could've sworn . . ." He shook his head. "I don't get it."

"And neither do I." In her agitation Torie began to pace the kitchen. "This house is so important to him. Why on earth would he give it up now that it's almost ready to occupy? This doesn't make sense."

Again Jerry shook his head. "Maybe I'd better talk to him."

"You have his phone number in Wilkesboro?" Torie demanded, clutching his arm.

"He's already left for the race?"

Torie released her death grip and sighed. Obviously Jerry was going to be no help at all. "This morning. Said he'd be back in two or three weeks and we'd work out the details of the sale then."

"But I thought he was going to...this just doesn't make sense."

"Isn't that what I just said?" Torie raged in exasperation.

Jerry rubbed his chin, clearly baffled. "Apparently he slept here last night. I wonder if that has anything to do with his decision."

"Slept *here?*"

Jerry shrugged. "His gear is in the bedroom. At least, I assumed it was his." Pivoting, Jerry led the way down the hall. He stepped into the room and pointed to an olive green sleeping bag, the kind used by the military.

Torie dropped to her knees beside it, running her hands over the thickly padded material. She spotted a crumpled shirt laying on the bag and snatched it up to her face. By inhaling deeply, she verified without a doubt who the owner was. Dan. There was no mistaking that potent masculine scent. Every hormone in her body leaped to attention.

"It's his," she confirmed, dropping it back on the bag. She then sat down next to it and peered up at her friend with a dejected sigh. Her bottom lip trembled. "Something's wrong. I just know it."

"Now don't get upset," Jerry told her. "I'm sure there's a logical explanation for everything." Though his words sounded positive, his expression showed his doubt, and Torie was not comforted. Her vision blurred with unshed tears.

"What do you think I should do?"

"Wait until he comes back, I guess," Jerry muttered.

"And what if he doesn't?"

Jerry tensed. "He will. Of course he will. That man is crazy in love with you, I mean *crazy.*"

"He is?"

"Hell, yeah, he is. And anyone can see you're in love with him. Yet he's off in Wilkesboro, risking his fool neck for a Winston Cup he won't want when he gets it, while you're sitting here moping in a stupid house you don't want now that you have it!" Huffing his frustration, Jerry glanced at his watch and muttered a colorful curse. "I've got to go pick Patty up and be at the bowling alley in Faulkner in twenty minutes. Are you going to be all right?"

"I'll be all right."

"Are you going to be home tomorrow?"

"Yes, why?"

"Because I've got a lecture that you're going to listen to, even if that mule-headed racer of yours didn't."

With that, Jerry stalked down the hall and out the front door, slamming it smartly behind him. Torie winced at the sound, which echoed through the empty house. Sniffing occasionally, she sat without moving a muscle for what must have been a long time since moonlight streamed through the windows when she became aware of her surroundings again.

Torie dried her eyes and got to her feet. Using the moon's glow, she perused the freshly painted area. When checking out the bathroom, now equipped with a modern shower unit and marble sinks. Torie next headed down the hall to the living room, where the smell of varnish, paint and new wood assailed her. Marveling that she hadn't noticed the scent before, Torie wrinkled her nose and climbed the stairs to inspect the bedrooms and the extra bath. They all looked ready for occupancy and she tried to envision herself actually making use of them.

But she could not, a development that startled and intrigued her. Was Jerry right? Did she *not* want the house now that she as good as had it?

Baffled, Torie stepped out into the upstairs hall and glanced at the entrance to her dad's old office. The broken pull had been replaced by a new one, which she could reach with ease. Torie raised her hand, lowering the door and then the ladder. Carefully she climbed up the enclosure.

It was quite dark in the room, since the window was so small. Torie didn't need light to know what the area looked like, however, and after walking around the familiar room she sat exactly where she and Dan had once sat, at the edge of the opening with her feet dangling over the hallway below.

Unbidden, memories washed over her—memories of that morning when they came so close to loving. Goose bumps danced over her bare arms. Torie closed her eyes, wondering at the closeness of body and spirit they had shared then and so many times since.

She tried to imagine how it would feel never to experience that oneness again and caught her breath at the loneliness that immediately gripped her. Awed by the intensity of it, Torie came to realize that if a million suitors knocked on her door, she would never find a man she loved as much as Dan Stewart.

He was life. He was happiness. He was forever.

And he was gone.

Blinded by new tears, Torie eased over to the steps and scooted down them on her backside so she wouldn't trip in the dark. She groped her way along the shadowy hall, down the stairs and then down the other hall until she once more reached the master bedroom. There, she threw herself on the sleeping bag and clutched Dan's shirt to her pounding heart.

What a fool she'd been to throw away a lifetime of happiness for an outdated dream. Millions of wives survived and functioned without their husbands beside them every minute—wives of truck drivers, pilots, military men. Surely she was woman enough to do the same.

It would take gumption. It would take guts. It would take the grace of God.

And it would require trading in an old dream for a newer model.

Faced with the stark reality of a lifetime without Dan, Torie realized she was more than ready for such a swap, whether or not Dan cared as much as Jerry said he did. The way Torie figured it, if Dan had not yet fallen in love with her, he soon would. She intended to make sure of that.

And his free-fall would be a thrill the likes of which no auto race could ever rival.

Smiling softly, Torie rolled onto her back and stared out the window at the full moon. Lost in new dreams and schemes, she inhaled the scent of Dan's shirt again and then wished on a star for its owner.

Her wish did not come true, of course, but Torie knew it soon would. Come tomorrow, she intended to pack her bags and follow Dan to Wilkesboro. She would be there when he raced, and she would take great pleasure in showing him that whether he finished first or not, he would always be a winner in her eyes.

Secure in the knowledge that she had finally found her forever after, Torie closed her eyes for just a moment, giving into her exhaustion. And though fully intending to hop right back up so she'd get home in time for Jerry's lecture—a lecture she no longer needed but was dying to hear—Torie dozed.

Dan drove home from Knoxville as though the demons that had haunted him since his goodbye to Torie were still on his tail. More than once during the day, his mother had commented on his blue mood, receiving nothing for her efforts but a mumbled excuse about the stress of the upcoming race.

The race was not the problem, of course, and Dan's blue mood was now black.

Furious with himself for his inability to come to terms with a choice that had been made for the best, Dan sped over the remaining miles to the trailer park. He fully intended to pack up, hook up and leave England tonight. There was no sense in prolonging the inevitable agony by waiting another moment.

And once safe in Wilkesboro, he would call Jerry regarding the final stages of restoration and, while he was at it, find out from Patty what he needed to do to sell the house. There was no reason to speak to Torie ever again, no reason, at all.

His mind on his property, Dan glanced absently at the place as he passed it, en route to England. He spied Torie's car out front and hit the brake of his truck, skidding to a stop. Luckily there were no other cars on the road—it was nearly midnight—and Dan sat for a moment, wondering what she was doing at the house at that hour.

Was she so anxious to get her hooks into it that she would spend the night without electricity or furniture? Probably, he decided with a disgusted snort, ignoring a niggling reminder that he had done exactly that not twenty-four hours earlier.

At once outrage washed over him—outrage that while he mourned the death of his dreams, she rejoiced in the rebirth of hers.

Fueled by his ire, Dan backed his truck and turned into the drive. He stalked from the truck to the porch, not even thinking about what he would say to Torie when he found her. All that mattered was that the house was not hers yet. She had no right to be there.

The interior was dark, except for the patchy squares of moonlight that streamed through the windows and illuminated the floors. Instinctively Dan headed straight for the master bedroom where he'd slept the night before. He burst through the door, nearly stumbling over his own feet when he found Torie stretched out on his forgotten sleeping bag, apparently deep in slumber.

Bathed in moonbeams, she was more bewitching than ever. Dan caught his breath, and awed by the sight, dropped to his knees within inches of where she lay. Silvery blond, her hair spilled over his pillow in wild disarray. On her cheek sparkled a single tear. Resisting the urge to touch it, Dan sat back on his heels and let his adoring gaze sweep her from head to toe.

Beautiful, he thought, his heart swelling with love so intense it actually hurt. Beautiful.

Almost immediately regret washed over him—regret that the feelings he'd finally acknowledged would never be returned. At once, Dan knew that if Torie would only admit to loving him a little he would give up everything for her. Nothing in this world—not the house, not the racing—was more important to him.

Dan let his gaze linger on her face, so youthful in repose, then lowered it. He saw that she held something clutched tightly in her hands, and tensed when he realized it was his shirt.

She hugged the garment as though it were something precious, and touched to his aching heart with the knowledge, Dan came to understand that he'd just received the admission of love he so desperately needed.

"Dan?" Though whisper soft, Torie's words startled him, and he jumped. Eyes open wide now, she reached out, as if to verify he was flesh and blood. Squealing her delight, she then threw herself into his waiting arms.

Without words, they promised eternity, and the moon paled in comparison to the glow of their love as a house became a home once again.

Epilogue

Torie placed a kiss on the almost-shaved chin of her husband of three years and then hugged him tight. Sighing her contentment with the roaring blaze in the fireplace at their feet and the handmade quilt spread on the wooden floor beneath them, she again congratulated herself on a brilliant decision. Anniversaries were so much more fun when celebrated in private. Why, a couple could do all sorts of things at home that they couldn't do in a crowded restaurant. Things like . . .

"What are you doing?" she gasped when Dan suddenly tugged upward on the hem of the nightie he'd bought as an anniversary present for both of them.

"Helping you out of this thing," he replied.

"But I just put it on."

He grinned. "I know. I helped."

"Some help you were," Torie grumbled, blushing as she remembered exactly *how* he'd helped.

Dan laughed good-naturedly and turned on his back, hands locked under his head. "So what would you rather do instead? I'm at your service."

Torie scanned his lean body, gloriously naked except for sinfully brief skivvies. With effort she dragged her eyes away. "I want to talk," she impishly suggested.

"Talk?" He moved just enough to nuzzle her neck.

"Yes . . . while I have your undivided attention." Torie eased away from Dan with reluctance and sat up, fully aware that her hot-blooded husband could see straight through the sheer fabric of the daring nightie. His immediate groan told her that he appreciated her efforts.

"Talk?" He traced the length of her bare legs with a forefinger, ankle to thigh.

"Uh-huh," she replied, playfully slapping at the fingers now reaching out to touch her breast. "I have something on my mind, something we need to discuss. You were so tired after last Sunday's race that you were almost sick. I mentioned it to Pete, and he hinted that maybe you weren't getting enough sleep the night before."

That got Dan's attention. "Oh, he did, did he?"

"Yes. So I was thinking that maybe we should, um, abstain on those nights—"

With a colorful curse, Dan rolled over, pinning Torie full beneath him. He then vetoed her teasing suggestion with a kiss so fiery she feared she would melt into a puddle of molten lava. "Any more bright ideas?" he asked long minutes later.

Torie sighed with satisfaction and shook her head. "No, but I think I should warn you that this kind of behavior might get you into trouble."

"Oh?"

"In fact, it already has. Thank goodness the season will be over a couple of weeks earlier than usual this year."

It was Dan's turn to sit up. He propped his elbow on the quilt and peered down at her. "What...are...you...talking...about?" he asked between kisses planted on several imaginative, astonishingly sensitive parts of her anatomy.

"Me," Torie somehow managed to gasp. "You. October twentieth."

He pulled back slightly, frowning. "What's happening October twentieth?"

"Well, if Dr. Frederick Larson knows his stuff, we're having a baby."

Silence followed her announcement. Then the walls of their home echoed with Dan's whoop of delight. He captured her in a bear hug.

"You do realize I won't be able to go to every race with you next season?" Torie asked softly against his chest. The past three years traveling the circuit with her handsome husband had been more wonderful than either had dared hoped they would be. She didn't know how Dan would feel about this new development.

"I do," he admitted after a moment of silence. "And while we're on the subject of next year, I, um, have a confession to make. I got a phone call yesterday from the program director for NSN."

"The sports network?" Torie asked. "What did he want?"

"He wants me to be an announcer for the NASCAR races they televise every Sunday. He's talking big bucks."

Torie caught her breath. "And how do you feel about that?"

"How do *you* feel about it?" Dan asked, instead of replying.

Torie sensed Dan's nervousness. She searched his face in silence for a moment, trying to read his thoughts. She saw worry. She saw indecision. She saw love.

Eternal love—that would be hers no matter what she asked of him. And for that reason, she knew what her answer had to be.

"Would you mind terribly if I told you I'd rather be married to a racer?" Torie asked, as certain she didn't want him to quit as she was that he would actually do it for her.

Dan tensed as though he couldn't believe his ears. *"You would?"*

"I would."

"Are you sure, babe?"

"Very, very sure," she told him.

The tension drained from his body, and he sagged against her, sighing his relief. "Thanks, Torie."

"My pleasure. And now that we've finally got that settled, tell me whether you want a boy or a girl."

"A girl," he answered without hesitation. "A towheaded baby girl who'll grow up to play in the backyard, wave at tourist trains and steal her future husband's heart, just like her mother."

"I did that?"

"Yes, indeed," he said with a brisk nod.

"Why on earth didn't you tell me before?"

"It's a long story."

"I'm yours forever," she reminded him softly.

Dan smiled at that, a tender smile that told her he'd always come back to make sure.

* * * * *

HARDEN

Diana Palmer

In her bestselling LONG, TALL TEXANS series, Diana Palmer brought you to Jacobsville and introduced you to the rough and rugged ranchers who call the town home. Now, hot and dusty Jacobsville promises to get even hotter when hard-hearted, woman-hating rancher Harden Tremayne has to reckon with the lovely Miranda Warren.

The LONG, TALL TEXANS series continues! Don't miss HARDEN by Diana Palmer in March . . . only from Silhouette Romance.

LTT-1

SILHOUETTE'S "BIG WIN" SWEEPSTAKES RULES & REGULATIONS

NO PURCHASE NECESSARY TO ENTER OR RECEIVE A PRIZE

1. To enter the Sweepstakes and join the Reader Service, scratch off the metallic strips on all your BIG WIN tickets #1-#6. This will reveal the potential values for each Sweepstakes entry number, the number of free book(s) you will receive and your free bonus gift as part of our Reader Service. If you do not wish to take advantage of our Reader Service but wish to enter the Sweepstakes only, scratch off the metallic strips on your BIG WIN tickets #1-#4. Return your entire sheet of tickets intact. Incomplete and/or inaccurate entries are ineligible for that section or sections of prizes. Torstar Corp. and its affiliates are not responsible for mutilated or unreadable entries or inadvertent printing errors. Mechanically reproduced entries are null and void.
2. Whether you take advantage of this offer or not, on or about April 30, 1992, at the offices of Marden-Kane Inc., Lake Success, NY, your Sweepstakes numbers will be compared against the list of winning numbers generated at random by the computer. However, prizes will only be awarded to individuals who have entered the Sweepstakes. In the event that all prizes are not claimed, a random drawing will be held from all qualified entries received from March 30, 1990 to March 31, 1992, to award all unclaimed prizes. All cash prizes (Grand to Sixth), will be mailed to the winners and are payable by check in U.S. funds. Seventh prize will be shipped to winners via third-class mail. These prizes are in addition to any free, surprise or mystery gifts that might be offered. Versions of this Sweepstakes with different prizes of approximate equal value may appear at retail outlets or in other mailings by Torstar Corp. and its affiliates.
3. The following prizes are awarded in this sweepstakes: ★ Grand Prize (1) $1,000,000; First Prize (1) $25,000; Second Prize (1) $10,000; Third Prize (5) $5,000; Fourth Prize (10) $1,000; Fifth Prize (100) $250; Sixth Prize (2,500) $10; ★★ Seventh Prize (6,000) $12.95 ARV.

   ★ This presentation offers a Grand Prize of a $1,000,000 annuity. Winner will receive $33,333.33 a year for 30 years without interest totalling $1,000,000.

   ★★ Seventh Prize: A fully illustrated hardcover book published by Torstar Corp. Approximate Retail Value of the book is $12.95.

   Entrants may cancel the Reader Service at anytime without cost or obligation to buy (see details in center insert card).
4. This Sweepstakes is being conducted under the supervision of an independent judging organization. By entering this Sweepstakes, each entrant accepts and agrees to be bound by these rules and the decisions of the judges, which shall be final and binding. Odds of winning in the random drawing are dependent upon the total number of entries received. Taxes, if any, are the sole responsibility of the winners. Prizes are nontransferable. All entries must be received at the address printed on the reply card and must be postmarked no later than 12:00 MIDNIGHT on March 31, 1992. The drawing for all unclaimed Sweepstakes prizes will take place on May 30, 1992, at 12:00 NOON, at the offices of Marden-Kane, Inc., Lake Success, New York.
5. This offer is open to residents of the U.S., the United Kingdom, France and Canada, 18 years or older, except employees and their immediate family members of Torstar Corp., its affiliates, subsidiaries, and all the other agencies, entities and persons connected with the use, marketing or conduct of this Sweepstakes. All Federal, State, Provincial and local laws apply. Void wherever prohibited or restricted by law. Any litigation within the Province of Quebec respecting the conduct and awarding of a prize in this publicity contest must be submitted to the Régie des Loteries et Courses du Québec.
6. Winners will be notified by mail and may be required to execute an affidavit of eligibility and release, which must be returned within 14 days after notification or an alternate winner will be selected. Canadian winners will be required to correctly answer an arithmetical skill-testing question administered by mail, which must be returned within a limited time. Winners consent to the use of their names, photographs and/or likenesses for advertising and publicity in conjunction with this and similar promotions without additional compensation. For a list of our major prize winners, send a stamped, self-addressed ENVELOPE to: WINNERS LIST, c/o Marden-Kane Inc., P.O. Box 701, SAYREVILLE, NJ 08871. Requests for Winners Lists will be fulfilled after the May 30, 1992 drawing date.

If Sweepstakes entry form is missing, please print your name and address on a 3″ ×5″ piece of plain paper and send to:

In the U.S.
Silhouette's "BIG WIN" Sweepstakes
3010 Walden Ave.
P.O. Box 1867
Buffalo, NY 14269-1867

In Canada
Silhouette's "BIG WIN" Sweepstakes
P.O. Box 609
Fort Erie, Ontario
L2A 5X3

Offer limited to one per household.

LTY-S391D